EVERY
BOSS
HAS A
Soft Spot
2

D1502802

A NOVEL BY

DANIELLE MAY

ACKNOWLEDGEMENTS & DEDICATION

First, I would like to give glory to God for presenting me with such an incredible opportunity. I would have never thought of having a career as an author, but you had it in your will. Thank you for giving me an amazing gift as well as allowing me to discover it. Whenever I'm doubting myself, I have a talk with you, and you come through for me each time, giving me the strength to move forward.

To my friends, it's so much that I can say about y'all, but I want to give a special thanks to Ashley. There have been times where I wanted to stop because I compared myself to other authors, but it was you who encouraged me to keep doing what I was doing and to always stay true to who I was. Thank you for being the realest friend that I have.

To the readers, thank you for giving me a chance. I appreciate everyone that took the time out of their lives just to read it. That means so much to me. I will continue to put out content that will hopefully keep you guys entertained and wanting more. Thank you so much. Be on the lookout for part two! It'll be out shortly.

CONTACT ME:

Facebook: Danielle May

Email: Labryar93@gmail.com

Snapchat: labryar93

PREVIOUSLY

Sasha

J was lying on my couch with all the lights in my house off except the TV screen. I was in the middle of watch *Waiting to Exhale* with a big bowl of chocolate ice-cream and a bag of vanilla cookies. I was watching the scene where Russell had come to Robin's house after being with his wife.

"You don't need him, with his trifling ass!" I yelled at the screen like they could really hear me. I was still in my feelings over Ron, but I was slowly—and I did mean slowly—trying to get over them. It had been three days since he basically told me we couldn't be together, and I walked out of his life. There were times that I wanted to text him, but I fought my urge. It was hard, trying to detox someone out of your system that was not only your first, but y'all had built a friendship as well. After we finished having sex, he would hold me and talk to me until we fell asleep. There had been plenty of times that he spent the night and even bought me breakfast so I wouldn't be hungry at work. It was the little things that made me fall in love with him, not just his sex. I was starting to get to know the real him, but it seemed as if he didn't want that, so it was best I ended whatever we had.

A knock at my door tore my eyes away from the movie. I got up and opened the door. Shawn walked in behind me. "What you got going on over here? I feel like I just walked into a 'no man allowed' zone." He gestured toward the movie and the snacks I was eating.

I moved my blanket off the sofa so he could have somewhere to sit down. "I'm just chilling," I said, patting the cushion beside me.

He took a seat and watched the movie with me. "I just don't understand men. Y'all have these perfectly good women chasing behind y'all, but y'all don't notice them until someone else want them," I vented.

"Don't say y'all, because every man ain't the same, just like every woman not. If I knew I had a good woman chasing after me, it wouldn't be any chasing. She would already be my woman."

I gave him a 'nigga, please' look. "I don't believe that, Shawn. Niggas be all confused about their feelings until they see that woman moving on, trying to be happy with someone else, then all of a sudden, they want to be with her," I replied, rolling my eyes with a cookie in my mouth.

"If a man really wants a woman, he will make it known. The woman wouldn't have to guess how he feels about her. The men you came across weren't really men; they were just boys." He used the same tone he used that day at the mall like there was a message hidden in there for me to decode.

I felt my phone vibrating and saw Tori's name pop up on the screen. She probably didn't want anything but to know what I was doing, so I silenced my phone and made a mental note to call her back once Shawn left.

Sitting my phone on the table, we finished watching the rest of the movie in silence. Once it was over, I leaned my head on the back of the pillows and stretched out my arms. I looked at Shawn and noticed that throughout the rest of the movie, he wore a serious expression.

"A penny for your thoughts?" I smiled, using the same words he used on me.

He let out a deep breath before gazing me in the eyes. "I don't know how you are going to react to what I tell you, but I need to get this off my chest. Remember when I told you a couple months before the wedding that I started to have doubts about getting married to her? The reason behind those doubts was you."

My eyes widened in disbelief.

"I have been in love with you since high school. You are the only person that didn't judge me based off my appearance and took the time out to know me. I wanted to tell you since our junior year how I felt, but I never had the courage to do so, fearing that you would reject me. Once we graduated and both moved to different states, I thought I had lost my chance, so I began trying to date. My ex reminded me of you a little. Y'all had the same wild, curly hair, body type, and couldn't dance for shit, but that's where the comparisons stopped. She was a taker, and you are a giver. You are caring and loving even to people that don't deserve it. That's one of the reasons I fell in love with you."

I sat there, speechless. Shawn had been my friend for years, and I never even had a clue that he felt this way about me, or maybe there were signs, and I just didn't want to see any. Knowing that I still had feelings for Ron, I didn't know how to respond to him. Maybe if he would've come back before Ron and I became close, then yes, I would've been with Shawn's sexy ass. Sadly, that wasn't the case.

Just when I was about to speak, he planted his lips on mine. My initial reaction was to push him off, but then something came over me, and I closed my eyes and kissed him back. Maybe Shawn was who I really needed, and Ron was just a distraction.

When I finally opened my eyes, I noticed the screen on my phone lighting up with Tori's name. Breaking our kiss, I grabbed my phone and accepted the call.

"Hey, what's—"

Before I could finish, she cut me off. "I've been trying to call you for almost an hour! You need to come to the hospital now! Ron has been in an accident!" she yelled through the phone.

As soon as the words left her mouth, everything around me went black.

Sasha

I could see Shawn's lips moving, but I couldn't hear a word he was saying. My mind was still trying to process the news Tori just laid on me. I literally felt like all the wind had been knocked out of my body.

"Accident? Is he going to be okay?" Jumping up of the couch, I paced back and forth in my living room. I felt a bunch of different emotions at this moment, but there were only two that stood out—fear and concern. Was it serious? Would he be okay? Those were the questions that circled around my mind. I knew I said that I didn't want anything to do with him, but I didn't want him out of my life prematurely either. Even though we ended on bad terms, I still cared about him. Feelings just didn't go away overnight.

"I don't know yet. We have been sitting in this waiting room for damn near an hour, and the doctor still hasn't come back and told us shit." She let out a deep sigh. "I had to calm Justin crazy ass down twice because he threatened to shoot up the place if they didn't let us know something soon."

"I'm on my way," I said, hanging up the phone. I walked into my room, frantically searching for a pair of shoes. Once I located a pair, I quickly put them on, grabbed my car keys off the dresser, and was headed straight to the door.

"What's going on? Are you okay? Talk to me," Shawn said, standing in the middle of the living room floor, his voice laced with concern. I was so worried about getting to the hospital that I had completely forgotten that Shawn was still here.

"I have to go. My friend got into an accident, and I need to make sure that he will be alright," I said in a rush, opening the door.

"I can come with you if you want. You don't look like you're in any condition to drive," he said, following behind me.

He might have been right, but there was no way that I would allow him to come with me to check up on somebody that I still had feelings for right after he just confessed his feeling for me. That would've been disrespectful on so many levels. "No, I'm good, but I really need to go."

He looked like he wanted to protest but decided against it. "Well, just call me when you get there so I can at least know that you made it there safely," he said, walking over to give me a hug.

Once he released me, I rushed to my car, heading straight to the hospital.

"God, please let Ron be okay. I know that I said that I didn't want him in my life anymore, but I didn't mean it. If you could do me this one favor, I promise that I will start reading the bible more and be a better person. Just please let him be okay," I prayed as I drove to the hospital, trying to wipe away the tears from my eyes, but it was no use.

I had done a good job of concealing my tears in the presence of Shawn, but now that I was alone, I couldn't fight them anymore. I didn't want to either. As much as I wiped, they continued to flow freely down my face. My vision was becoming blurry, so I pulled over to the side of the road. Covering my face with my hands, I laid my head on the steering wheel and cried my heart out. I heard people say that crying was a cleanser to the soul, and I was giving mine a thorough one.

I couldn't even fathom the thought of never being able to hear his voice or see him again. Sure, he was selfish and inconsiderate, but I didn't want my last words to him be goodbye. Why was it that a person that came into my life in the most obnoxious way could mean so much to me in less than a year? I was with Kendrick for three years, and I never felt this strongly for him. Why did this have to happen to him when I was doing my best of trying to move on? It seemed like every time I tried to distance myself from him, the universe found a way to pull me back to him.

After crying for a few more minutes, I finally pulled myself together and wiped my face off with a napkin I found in the glove compartment. I pulled down the sun visor and opened the mirror to check my appearance. My eyes were still puffy from crying, and my nose was a little red, but other than that, I was good.

Just when I was about to put my car back in drive, I heard my phone ringing. I quickly answered once I saw who it was. "Did y'all finally get an update on his condition?"

"From what the doctor says, he has a bruised rib and a deep gash on his left side that caused him to lose a lot of blood. They had to give him a blood transfusion and stitch him up, but other than that, he will be alright."

Letting out a sigh of relief, I silently thanked God. I was happy that he was going to be okay. "Are y'all still there?"

"Yes, but we are about to leave. His mom told us that we can leave and come back tomorrow because he is passed out from all that medication they doped him up with. Where are you at?"

"I was almost at the hospital before you called, but I am about to turn around and go back home now that I know that he is fine."

"Okay, I'mma call you tomorrow so we can hang out. I need a damn break from this stupid ass nigga. He 'bout three seconds away from me stabbing his ass. Don't you know he had the nerve to look at one of those nurse's asses while we were sitting in the waiting room? I wanted to light his ass up, but due to the circumstances, I couldn't. But best believe he is gon' hear my mouth about it," she said, giving me a much-needed laugh for today.

It was always something with those two. "Just give me a heads up before you do anything so I can have your bail money ready."

"I knew you were my nigga for a reason, but let me get off this phone because I see him coming this way."

"Alright," I said before she hung up.

Leaning back in the seat, I debated whether or not I should turn back around and head home or go to the hospital to see him. I knew that Tori said he was fine, and I didn't doubt that she was telling the truth, but in order for me to sleep tonight, I needed to see him with my own eyes, especially since I didn't know when I would see or talk to him after tonight. Giving in to my urge, I pulled off and headed straight to the hospital.

Once I arrived, I went to the front desk and asked the nurse what room Ron was in. After she gave me the information, I thanked her and made a beeline to the elevator. I pushed the floor number and laid my head against the wall. Closing my eyes, I took a deep breath then exhaled, trying to calm down my nerves. When the door opened, I took my time walking down the hall. I became more and more nervous with every step I took.

Finally making it to the room number that the nurse gave me, I placed my hand on the doorknob, but for some reason, I couldn't bring myself to turn it. I just stood there, contemplating on what my next move should be. I knew I said I wanted to see him, but now that the only thing that was standing in between that happening was a door, I was scared—scared of what type of condition I would see him in and if I would be strong enough to walk away from him this time.

Taking a deep breath, I found enough strength to turn the knob, slowly opening the thick wooden door. Once I fully entered the room, I walked over to him and froze in place as I watched him sleeping peacefully. How could seeing him still have the same effect on me after all this time? Every time I laid eyes on him, it was like the butterflies in my stomach got active.

My eyes roamed all over his body, examining him. His once flawless, honey-brown complexion looked dull. There were a few bruises on his face, but they didn't take away from his sexiness, and his dreads were all over his head. I couldn't help myself as I removed one of the dreads that rested over his left eye. I smiled, looking at the frown that he wore on his face as he slept. I would bet money that even in his dreams, he was being an asshole to someone.

My smile slowly started to fade when I thought about our last encounter and how he had made it perfectly clear that there would never be anything between us. I could still hear his words echoing in my head. *If you want to walk away from me, then go. I don't know what else you want from me.* I had to be real with myself and let the little bit of hope I had for us go. Right in that moment, I made the decision that once I left out of this room, I would be moving on with my life. I refused to sit around and wait for a man to decide if he wanted to be with me or not when I had a perfectly good one that made it known that he wanted to be in my life.

I was so caught up in my thoughts that I didn't notice that somebody had come into the room until I heard someone clearing their throat behind me.

I slowly turned around and laid eyes on a very pretty woman with a short hairdo. I noticed that she had the same golden complexion and hazel eyes as Ron. It only took me a second to realize that this woman had to be his mother. My anxiety kicked in upon my realization.

"It seems like you were in deep thought over there," his mother said, walking over to the other side of Ron's bed and fixing the blankets on him. Once she was done, she looked over to me, waiting for me to respond.

I shifted uncomfortably as she stared at me. "I, umm… It was nothing. I heard about the accident and came to see how he was doing," I stuttered.

"It had to be something if you didn't hear me come in the room," she said, finally smiling. "I don't think I've had the pleasure of meeting you. My name is Mary, and you are?"

"I'm sorry. My name is Sasha," I said, reaching my hand out for her to shake, which she accepted.

"It's nice meeting you, Sasha. So how are you and my son associated with one another?" she inquired with a curious look on her face.

I thought about it for a minute. "I guess you can say that we were somewhat friendly with each other," I replied. That was the best way I could think of to describe our situation, or lack thereof.

"Were?" She raised an eyebrow. "Hmm… that's interesting. When I walked in on you a few minutes ago, with the way you were looking at him, I would have thought that it was something more than just being *friendly* with each other, but what do I know about y'all younger generation?" She smiled at me before returning her gaze back to Ron.

I looked on as I saw her gently fluffing the pillow behind his head. I could see the love that she had for her son in her eyes. I remembered having a conversation with Ron about his mother a couple a weeks ago while we lay in bed together. He was telling me how although he and his father were close, he felt closer to his mother even though she could be overbearing sometimes.

I looked at my phone, noticing that it was close to one in the morning, and I had to be up in less than eight hours. "Well, I should get going. I have to work in a couple of hours. I just came by to check on Ron and see if he was okay. It was nice meeting you, Mrs. Carter." I waved, turning to leave.

She stopped me in my tracks and pulled me into a hug. "It was nice meeting you too. I hope to see you around more," she said, releasing me from the hug.

I didn't want to tell her that I highly doubted she would see me again, so I simply nodded my head in response, making my exit.

When I finally made it home, I texted Shawn, letting him know that I had made it in safe and that I would catch up with him later on this week. Walking into my bedroom, I searched through my drawer, trying to find something that I could change in for bed. Slipping off the clothes that I had on and putting on my sleeping clothes, I got in bed.

Closing my eyes, I tried to find sleep, but after twenty minutes of tossing and turning, I snatched the covers off my body and headed to my painting room. I went over to my painting board and poured different colors of paint in the small circular holes, careful not to waste anything on the floor. Next, I placed the canvas on the stand and grabbed a painting brush off the dresser in front of me. I started painting, entering a world where I didn't have to feel hurt, sadness, pain, or rejection—a world where I was numb to everything.

Ron

I was in the middle of playing a basketball game when suddenly, my mother burst through the door and turned off the TV.

"Aye, what's up? What you do that for!" I yelled, glaring at her. I was already pissed off at the fact that she forced my ass to come and stay at her and my dad's house. That slow ass doctor told her I needed someone to watch me the first couple days I was out of the hospital because I wouldn't be able to do certain stuff for myself. And now she was coming in here, turning off my shit. I had only been here for a day, and I was already ready to leave from this bitch. I would've preferred to stay at my own damn house, but she claimed that was too far of a drive for her to do every day.

"You have been locked in this room, playing these video games since you got discharged from the hospital yesterday. Didn't the doctor tell you that you should start moving around so you can heal quicker?" she scolded me, walking over to the curtains, opening them, letting the sunlight shine through.

I put my hands over my eyes until my eyes could adjust to the light. Taking a deep breath, I ran my hands down my face before I looked in her direction. "It's only nine in the morning, Ma, and I know you don't think that I'm about to go outside this early in the cold?" She was out of her mind if she thought I was about to do that shit.

"No, but I do expect you to walk downstairs with me so I can fix you something to eat. Now, get up. You know I didn't raise you to lay around in bed all day."

She pulled the covers from my body, and I slowly sat up. I groaned a little from the pain of the cut on my side. I wasn't going to lie; it hurt like a bitch, but I pushed through it. Once we finally made to the downstairs living room area, my mother helped me get comfortable on the couch and headed to the kitchen to cook breakfast. I felt my phone vibrating in my gym shorts, so I pulled it out and answered it.

"What's up?" I said into the phone.

"Shit, nothing. I was calling to check up on you," Justin said.

"My whole fucking body is sore, but other than that, I'm good," I said, grabbing the remote so I could turn on the TV.

"I'm about to pull up on you in a few. You still at Ma Duke house?"

I frowned up my face. "Where else would I be at? You know she ain't letting me leave until I can moonwalk out this bitch." We shared a laugh.

"Yeah, true that, but I'll be there in about thirty minutes."

"Aight," I said, hanging up the phone.

I was watching an old episode of *The Bernie Mac Show* when my mother brought a big ass plate of food and a glass of orange juice to me. I grabbed the plate and placed it on my lap before I said my grace and started digging in.

"So how are you feeling?" she asked, sitting down on the opposite end of the couch I was sitting on.

"I'm good, Ma. In a couple of days, I'll be back to normal," I said, stuffing my mouth with more food.

"I was so worried when I got that call from the police telling me that you were in an accident. No parent wants to hear about something bad happening to their child. I don't know what I would've done if…" She shook her head before wiping her right eye.

"Don't think like that. I already told you before that I'm not tapping out before you," I joked, trying to comfort her.

"I'm just glad you are okay, but apparently, I'm not the only one that feels that way."

I looked in her direction with a raised brow. "What do you mean by that?" I questioned.

"While we were waiting to hear from the doctor, Amber came into the waiting room, crying and carrying on like she didn't have the sense that God gave her. A nurse had to come and threaten to put her out if she didn't stop keeping up that fuss."

Instantly, I got pissed off. She was starting to become a thorn in my fucking side. I had to make her disappear ASAP. First, she called my mother, lying about our arrangement. Then she went out of her way to find Sasha and feed her a bullshit ass story about being my girl. It still puzzled me how she even knew who Sasha was to confront her in the first place. Now she was coming to the hospital, making a fucking scene. That crazy bitch's days were numbered. I made a mental note to hit up one of the female workers and have them handle that for me.

"I hope you sent her on her way. I don't mess with her no more for her to be doing all that extra stuff."

"I did. I told her it would be best if she left, and I would call her once I knew something. I can't tell you how many missed calls and texts I got from her that night. I had to cut my phone off just to get some peace." She laughed, but I didn't find shit funny at all. If anything, that just told me that I needed to speed up the process of my plans. I'd seen women go crazy over niggas that they were in relationships with, or when you gave them a little bit of attention, they did some dumb shit, but Amber was taking it to a whole different level.

"Block her then. I told you to do that before, but you didn't listen. You don't need to be in contact with a person like that."

"From the way she carried on, I might just do that," she agreed before continuing on with the story. "Then, I had stepped out of your room for a minute to make a call, and when I came back, it was a girl standing at your bedside, and from the puffiness of her eyes, I could tell she had been crying. I think she said her name was Sasha."

Now that got my attention. I stopped mid-bite at the mention of Sasha's name. I hadn't heard or seen her since that conversation we had outside of the activity center that day. I would be lying if I said that a part of me was a little messed up because I did fuck with her the long way. She had me doing shit that usually wasn't in my nature, like spending the night with her after we got done fucking or staying up all night, watching movies, and just talking until the sun came up.

But I wasn't about to let her force me into something that I knew I wasn't ready for yet and that would potentially have her hating me in the end. I'd rather keep it how it was between us right now, and maybe later on in life, I'd get back up with her, and we could try that relationship shit. I wasn't worried about her finding another nigga. I knew that I had her heart, and if a nigga thought he could get that, then I would gladly kill his ass and then attend his funeral like I didn't do shit.

"Oh, that's what's up," I responded in a nonchalant voice, going back to eating my food.

I could feel my mother staring a hole through my face, but I ignored her, focusing on my food. "I asked her how y'all knew each other, and she told me that y'all were on 'friendly terms,' as she put it, but judging from her reaction and yours, something tells me that there's more to the story. Do you have any type of feelings for this girl?" she asked, awaiting my answer.

Handing her my empty plate so she could put it on the coffee table beside her, I took a long gulp of juice before answering. "She is a cool person. We were chilling with each other for a minute, doing our thing, but that's about it." I shrugged my shoulders, looking at the TV, letting her know that I didn't want to continue with this conversation.

Just when she opened her mouth to say something, the doorbell rang, which I was thankful for. She got up from the couch to open the door. Moments later, I heard Justin and Bryan's loud ass voices as they entered the house and greeted my mother.

"What's up, Ron, over there looking like a battered house husband with those scratches on your face," Justin joked, walking over, dapping me up.

"Fuck you with your ol' dusty-looking ass," I said, laughing.

"Boy, watch your mouth," my mother warned, hitting me on top of the head.

"He just so disrespectful. I know you raised him better than that," Bryan said, hugging her. "Every time I see you, you look younger and younger. What's your secret so I can give these girls out here some tips?"

She waved him off with a laugh. "Boy, you are so silly. If y'all need anything let me know." She walked out of the living room, giving us some privacy.

"So how the fuck did you get into an accident, my nigga?" Justin started off.

"Being for real, that shit is a blur to me. I'm still trying to figure it out my damn self. I was leaving from this new bitch that I'm fucking, and next thing I know, I hit something, and my car flipped over," I said, stroking my chin in thought.

"You don't think this was a setup, do you?" Bryan questioned.

I shook my head. "No, I don't." I had a sixth sense when I knew something was about to go down or if something wasn't right, but I didn't get that vibe at all. I just chalked this situation up as shit just happened sometimes.

"Aight, nigga, if you say so," he replied, ending the conversation. We spent the rest of the time going over our next business move, and they filled me in on what had been going on since my absence.

Bryan was the first to leave. "I'm about to head out," he said, standing up. "I'm about to let somebody daughter swallow all my children," he sang off-key. We laughed at that nigga as he headed out the door, throwing up the peace sign.

"You can't tell me he ain't gon' catch something that is gon' make his dick fall off one day with all the hoes he be fucking," Justin stated, shaking his head. I couldn't say anything about that nigga when I was basically out here doing the same thing. The only difference was a bitch had to meet my standards. I wasn't around here just giving my dick out like that, and I always strapped up. Bryan, on the other hand, would fuck anything with a pussy, no matter the face that was attached to it. That's how he got stuck with that ugly ass baby mama of his for the next eighteen years.

"Aye, have you heard from baby girl yet, or is she still not fucking with yo' ass?" He laughed, referring to Sasha.

I was starting to get irritated with people all of a sudden bringing up her name up. "What's up with y'all asking me about that girl? First my mama, and now you. I'll tell you just like I told her. No, I haven't heard from her, and I don't expect to either. We ain't fucking with each other on that level like that anymore. We had our lil' thing, and now the shit is over with. It is what it is, and I'm not sweating it. Point. Blank. Period," I told him. I didn't know who I was trying to convince more—him or myself.

He gave me the side eye. "Aight, nigga, if you say so." He looked as if he didn't believe me, but he dropped the subject. "But I'm about to take my ass to the barbershop so I can get me a line-up. My shit looking real raggedy right now," he said, moving, his hand up and down his head. "I'mma holla at you later with your crippled ass."

"Fuck you," I responded, laughing.

After he had left, I got up slowly from the couch, careful not to burst any of my stitches. The last thing I wanted to do was end back up in the hospital again. I decided to walk around this big ass house a minute because I wasn't about to go out in that cold ass weather anytime soon. I needed to get back to my old self, fast. I wasn't the type of nigga that felt comfortable lying around all damn day, not doing nothing. I was used to constantly moving around and doing things. That sitting around shit just didn't feel right to me. Plus, I had multiple business that I needed to tend to. Sure, I could handle it from home, but I was a hands-on type of nigga, and not to mention, I didn't trust people to handle my shit for me. Just thinking about that gave me enough motivation to walk around the entire house five times in a row.

Sasha

Twirling side to side in my chair with my headset resting on top of my head, I stared at the computer screen in front of me, daydreaming. It was another slow day at work, and I was extremely bored. I hated just sitting down with nothing to do because it only made the time go by slower. Since having our phones out wasn't allowed, I pulled out a puzzle book. Hopefully, this would make the next three hours go by fast. I was just about done finding the last word when I felt my phone vibrate in the hoodie that I wore. Looking over at my coworkers, making sure they weren't watching me, I discreetly pulled out my phone, opening the message.

Shawn: You have any plans for tonight?

Me: I was going to get some painting done, but other than that, no.

Shawn: I'm back in town and I wanted to know if you are down to go get something to eat since I haven't saw you in almost a month.

Me: I'm down. I'll call you when I make it home.

Shawn: Ok Bet

I placed my phone back in my hoodie with a smirk on my face. I was more than ready to get off now. The past few weeks, Shawn and I had gotten closer. Even though he went back to New York, we talked on the phone nearly every day and FaceTimed often. Even when he knew he would have a busy day, he made time to text and let me know, and he called me before I went to bed.

On the drive home after visiting Ron, I had an epiphany. Having a relationship with Shawn wouldn't be a bad idea. I wouldn't have to go through the whole process of getting to know him. He had been my best friend for the past seven years, and we pretty much knew all the things that there was to know about one another.

I didn't have to worry about if he really liked me for me, or if he was just pretending so he could get in my pants, because he wasn't that type of person. We knew each other's families, so I wouldn't have to worry about my family not liking him, and my mother already considered him as her son. I was happy to have my friend back in my life, and if he kept playing his cards right, he would be more than that pretty soon.

Once I was finally off, I texted Shawn as soon as I got in the car to let him know that I was on my way home so he could come over in about an hour. I hooked my AUX cord up to the radio, scrolling down until I landed on H.E.R's album and pressed play, vibing to her music all the way home. I made a beeline to my door as soon as I parked the car.

While I was opening the door, I heard a car playing some loud ass music while driving by. I turned in the direction of where it was coming from, and my heartbeat sped up a little when I saw Ron's car passing by. Just for a moment, I thought he was coming to see me, but when I saw him turn left, I knew that he was going to fuck that girl that lived in the other building from me. It hurt me a little to see him pass by and not even acknowledge me.

I quickly opened my door and slammed it shut. Feeling myself beginning to think about him, I quickly snapped out of it. I wasn't about to allow him to ruin my good mood. If he wanted to go through his life being a hoe, then that was on him.

I headed to the bathroom to take a quick shower before Shawn made it. Taking off my clothes and grabbing a towel, I stepped in, letting the hot water hit my skin, instantly soothing my body. I grabbed my Dove soap off the holder, lathering up the towel. I washed all over my body. After finishing up in the bathroom, I picked out a cute yet warm outfit to wear. I didn't have to worry about doing anything to my hair. I had done my hair in a braid-out yesterday, and my curls were still popping.

I heard a knock on my door, so I checked my appearance once more before turning off the lights and grabbing my purse. I opened the door and almost fainted when I saw Shawn standing there with a smile plastered on his face, looking fine as ever. Also, I was pleasantly surprised to see he no longer wore braces.

"What happened to your braces? I was getting used to seeing them on you," I said, locking the door behind me before giving him a hug. I didn't know what type of cologne he was wearing, but it smelled so good that I almost didn't want to let him go.

He laughed. "It was time for them to come off. I was only supposed to have them on for three years."

I followed behind him as he led the way to his car. He went over to the passenger side and held the door open for me and closed it once I was inside. Walking around to the other side, he got in, and we were off to our destination.

"So where exactly are we going to get something to eat?" I questioned, looking at the side of his face.

"That's up to you. What are you feeling right now?"

"I don't know why you ask me that. You know I can't ever decide on a place," I whined. I didn't know why men asked women what or where they wanted to get something to eat from when they knew that the answer would always be 'I don't know.'

"I knew you would say that. I only asked because I wanted to be considerate, but I got a place in mind that I know you are going to like." He smiled in my direction then turned his attention back at the road.

"You just think you know me, huh?" I teased.

He raised an eyebrow. "Is that a trick question or something? Girl, I know you like the back of my hands. You know you are the female version of me, so I don't see why you playing." He reached over to pinch my cheek, causing me to blush.

I playful pushed his hand from my face. "Yeah, whatever. Just concentrate on the road," I said, turning up the volume on the stereo. A couple of songs went by before I looked over at him and him back at me, giving each other knowing looks. I turned the volume all the way up when I heard Tupac "Hit 'Em Up" playing. It was our all-time favorite song. We went back and forth, rapping the verses to each other. This brought back memories of us being in the living room at my parents' house, blasting music, and dancing around until my mom shut it down.

He pulled into the parking lot of a Mexican restaurant, and I smiled in approval. I hadn't had Mexican food in a while, because I was trying to cut back on food that wasn't good for my body, but I was pretty sure eating a couple of tacos wouldn't hurt me. Once we were seated at our table, we ordered our drinks and food. I didn't have to look at the menu; I already knew what I wanted.

"I take it you approve of my choice in picking somewhere to eat?" he asked with a smirk on his face.

I playfully rolled my eyes. "I mean, it'll do. You could've picked a better place than this," I said with a shrug of the shoulders. When I saw his facial expression, I burst out laughing. "I'm just playing with you."

He let out a nervous chuckle. "You had me scared for a minute. I was about to suggest someplace else."

"No, this place is fine. You know I love tacos. I would eat them for the rest of my life if I could, but I would need someone pushing me. It's no way I'll be able to move around by myself."

"I would gladly push you around for a small fee. So what are you willing to pay me?" he asked in a suggestive tone. Immediately, my mind went straight to sex. I didn't know if he meant it like that, but that's how my horny ass mind took it.

I shifted in my seat a little and cleared my throat. "I knew you weren't a real friend," I replied, trying to play it cool.

The waiter came back with our drinks and food. I wasted no time biting into one of my tacos. I closed my eyes and let out a low moan as my taste buds were greeted by the delicious flavors. During the course of the meal, Shawn tried to make conversation, but I was so busy stuffing my face with the food that I didn't hear a word that he said. When I finally finished my last bite of taco, I leaned back in my seat, rubbing my stomach. I was so full that it felt like my belly was about to pop at any minute.

I watched Shawn as he waved over our waiter so we could get the check. "Have you had any luck with finding a paint dealer?

I let out an exaggerated sigh. "Not really. I mean, I went to a few, and they seemed like they might've been interested, but I haven't heard back from them." I was still considering moving back home next year if I didn't make any process with my painting, but until then, I was willing to exhaust all of my options.

"Don't worry about that. You are talented, and I'm positive you will catch your big break soon. Just keep doing what you are doing, and don't stop," he said with an encouraging smile.

I offered a lazy smile. "I hope you are right."

We sat in silence for a minute before Shawn spoke. "Are we going to continue to ignore the elephant in the room?" he asked me.

I raised my brows in confusion. "What are you talking about?"

"The last time I was here, I put my feelings out on the table, and we kissed, but you never told me how you felt about what I said."

I was a little caught off guard by his statement. I was starting to look at him as being more than just my friend, and I could see myself being with him. He was a good person to talk to, a great listener, and not to mention, he was a fine, successful Black man—everything that I knew I needed. But I still had lingering feelings for Ron. I didn't want to agree to be with him, knowing that my heart wouldn't fully be in it. That wouldn't be fair to either one of us.

"I don't know what to say." I swirled my straw around in my drink, trying to avoid looking him in the face. "I have given some thought to us being together as a couple, but I just don't want to jump into anything too soon, you know."

I finally looked in his direction to see if I could see his reaction. He sat there with a straight face, giving me no indication of how he felt. Seeing him giving me this face made Ron flash into my head. I always hated that I could never guess what was on his mind when he did this.

"I get where you are coming from. I don't want to make you feel like I'm pressuring you into something, so I'll take what I can get right now. Just don't have me waiting for long," he said, looking me in the eyes.

"I won't keep you waiting for long. I have to sort a few things out before I can agree to anything."

He paid for the meal, and we left. The ride back to my apartment was uncomfortable for me. I didn't know how he really felt about the answer I gave him. He seemed to be okay with it, but was that just an act? I didn't know. Maybe I was overthinking it. I found myself stealing glances at him as he drove. I took this time to really take him in.

His dark-chocolate complexion looked like smooth leather under the moonlight. The waves he rocked were on point, and it looked as if he'd just gotten a fresh line-up. The mustache and beard he rocked shaped his face perfectly. His lips were a little on the thin side, but they were still big enough to kiss on, and he had these dark-brown, bedroom eyes that I could easily see myself getting lost in. He was really a beautiful man that any woman would be lucky to have, and he was choosing me. I moved my hands toward his face and stroked his jawline, smiling.

He looked surprised by my action as he looked back and forth between the road and me. "What are you doing?" he asked with a grin surfacing on his face.

I could tell that he was enjoying it from his reaction. "I just felt like touching that sexy face of yours. Why? Do you want me to stop? Because I will." I smirked.

He said nothing as I continued to stroke the side of his face. Once we made it back to my apartment, he walked me to the door. This was another thing I liked about him. He was the definition of a true gentlemen.

"Thank you for walking me to the door and feeding me," I said, leaning my back against the door.

"No problem." We stood there for a few seconds, staring at one another. "I guess I'll let you go. I know you have to paint and get ready for work," he said, stuffing his hands in his pockets.

"Yeah, I better head on in." I turned to unlock the door, but something all of a sudden came over me. I turned back around and grabbed the back of Shawn's neck, pulling him in to a kiss. I could tell my aggressiveness caught him off guard, but he didn't pull away from the kiss. His tongue entered my mouth, and I gladly accepted it. We kissed for what seemed like hours, what in actuality was only minutes. I finally pulled away, using my thumb to wipe my lip gloss off his lips.

"Now I really better get going before we start something we won't be able to finish."

I toyed with the thought of having sex with him. It wouldn't be a bad idea. Since it had been close to a month and a half since I'd had sex, my hormones were out of control right now, but I had to think with my head and not my hormones.

"Yeah, you might be right." I opened the door and walked in. "Goodnight. Call me when you make it home."

"I have a few errands to run, but if I think you are sleep, I'll just text you." He walked up to me, giving me one last peck on the lips before telling me goodnight then walking away. I closed the door once I saw his car pulling off. I slid my body down the frame of the door, fanning myself. I thought it was safe to say that I liked him a little bit more now. Getting up from the floor, I walked to my bedroom, preparing my work clothes for tomorrow.

****

"You have to come out with me tonight. It's Justin's birthday, and you know all those thirsty ass hoes are gon' be on his dick. I need backup just in case one of them want to get out of line and try me," Tori begged, flopping down on the sofa near me.

I decided to stop by her house so we could hang out and chill, but now I was regretting my decision. "That gives me even more reason not to come. I don't have time to be up fighting. We are getting too old for that anyways," I said, smacking on some grapes in my mouth.

"Old?" she said, scrunching up her face. "Last time I checked, my fine ass wasn't old, and I don't see a problem with checking bitches that come near my man. And don't think I don't know the real reason why you don't want to come. Your scared ass thinks Ron is going to be there, don't you?" she questioned, playfully pushing me.

I hated the fact that she could see right through me. That was the exact reason why I didn't want to come. Ron and I had been doing a good job of staying out of each other's ways, and if I was being completely honest, I was happy about it. I had gotten to the point that he barely crossed my mind anymore, and I wanted to keep it that way. I was finally moving on with my life, and I didn't want to mess up my progress.

"Exactly. And you already know why, so you should understand why I can't go." I threw a grape in her direction.

She kissed her teeth. "You talking about us being too old to fight, but yo' ass is too old to be ducking and dodging a nigga that could care less about what you are doing. Didn't nobody tell you to let that nigga spread it wide, pull your panties to the side, and then give it to you," she sang, popping her butt on the sofa, causing both of us to laugh. "But on some real shit. I don't even know why you let that nigga be your first after I told you about his reputation with women."

"I know it was a stupid decision to make, but at the time, I thought that I could handle him—if that makes sense," I said, putting my head down.

Tori got up from her seat and hugged me. "Don't think that I'm judging you, because I'm not. We all make some stupid ass decisions in life. But if I'm honestly speaking, you are too good of a person to be dealing with his bipolar ass anyways." We sat in silence for a moment. "Sooo how was the dick?"

I pulled away from her and looked at her like she was crazy. "Did you really just ask me that?"

"What? I just wanted to know if his dick game is lethal like those hoes say it is. If his dick game is anything like Justin's, then I don't blame you for agreeing to that stupid shit y'all had going on," she said, shrugging up her shoulders like it wasn't a big deal.

I thought about it for a minute before a smirk formed on my face. "Let's just say that I was well satisfied."

"I knew it!" she screamed. "But luckily for you, Justin told me that Ron is out of town, so he won't be there tonight. Now you don't have an excuse to not come out."

"Okay, fine, but under two conditions. One, don't start no unnecessary shit tonight. Two, you have to promise me you won't get drunk." It was one thing dealing with her while she was sober, but it was another story when she got drunk. It was like she became even crazier than she already was.

"Okay, I promise."

"I'm coming." I rolled my eyes, finally giving in.

She screamed in excitement. "Yass, bitch! We are going to turn the fuck up tonight! The dress code is all-black, and the theme for tonight is Grown and Sexy. So you better show the fuck out."

I groaned. I didn't have any club attire to wear in my closet. Now I had to go out and buy an outfit.

The alarm system went off, and moments later, Justin appeared with a bunch of bags in his hands.

"What's up, ladies? What y'all doing over here?" he spoke, setting the bags down on the floor.

"Oh, hell nawl!" Tori yelled, walking up to him. "Why in the hell you left the house in some damn sweatpants, advertising your dick print and shit? You must want these hoes out here to know what you're working with?"

He stared at her for a second, frowning up his face. "Man, get on with that bullshit. Today is a nigga birthday, and I'm not 'bout to let you fuck up my mood, so sit yo' ass down somewhere," he said, brushing past her, going up the stairs.

"No, fuck that. You won't be happy until I have to kill one of these dirty bitches behind yo' Black ass. Matter fact, let me wear some tights and show off my pussy print since that's what we're doing now," she said, following behind him.

He stopped walking and turned around. "Do that shit and see won't I embarrass your ass in front of everybody." He glared at her before continuing to climb back up the stairs.

I took this as my cue to leave. I told them I was leaving, but I doubted that they heard me with all the screaming and yelling they were doing. After I left, I headed straight to the mall to find something to wear. Once I found an outfit that I thought fit the theme of the party, I went home to catch a few hours of sleep before the party.

I stared at myself in my full-length mirror, turning my body slightly around to get a better view of myself. This was definitely out of my comfort zone, but I must admit, I did look cute. I had on a black, strapless midriff top that exposed my stomach, a black skirt that stopped above my knees with a slit on the side, showing off my toned legs, and a pair of black, six-inch, open-toes heels.

I decided to straighten my hair at the last minute, so it was no longer in its natural state. My hair had grown tremendously since the last time I'd worn it straight, now stopping at middle of my back. I wanted to put some curls in my hair, but I opted to just wearing it down with a part on the side. I didn't have on much jewelry. Only a gold body chain and three gold bracelets decorated my right arm. Looking at the time, I saw that it was a little bit after midnight. Grabbing my clutch purse and perfume, I was out the door.

Pulling up to the club, I saw that there was a sea of people standing outside, and the line damn near circled around the building. I pulled out my phone and called Tori. I'd be damn if I was about to wait in this long ass line.

She didn't pick up the phone the first time, so I called her back. If she didn't answer the phone this time, I was leaving.

"Where are you at?" she yelled over the loud music in the background.

"I'm sitting outside in my car. There aren't any parking spaces, and it's a long line outside of the building."

"Drive around to the side of the building, and I'll meet you out there," she said before ending the call.

I did as she instructed and pulled around to the side of the building. I noticed that there was security standing next to a rope that was blocking me from entering. Just as I was about to call Tori back, I saw her come out the side door and whisper something in the security guard's ear. He removed the rope, and I drove in. I sprayed some perfume on myself and gave myself one last look before exiting the car. Once I felt the cool wind hit me, I instantly regretted not bringing a small jacket to cover up with.

"Look at you, looking all sexy and shit," Tori said as soon as I caught up with her. "And it look like yo' booty got bigger. Let me find out that Shawn's sexy ass been hitting that."

I giggled, waving her off. "Girl, please. Ain't nobody been hitting nothing, but you look pretty as well," I said, admiring her look.

Her dreads were in a braided up-do that was styled to perfection. She had on a black Prada mini dress with the back out. The dress was sexy but still classy, and to top it all off, a pair of six-inch red bottom heels graced her feet.

As soon as I stepped into the building, my mouth dropped. The party was lit as fuck. It seemed like everyone was there, from the rappers and athletes to the ballers of the city. And it was a known fact that wherever there was a bunch of paid niggas, there would be women dressed in the most whorish outfits, looking for their come up, and they were in full swing tonight.

There were security guards all around the place, I guess to make sure that nothing popped off tonight. Tori and I navigated through the crowd, walking hand in hand until we made it to the VIP section that towered over the dance floor. When the security guard saw us coming, he let us through the rope. I followed closely behind Tori as she made her way over to where Justin was rolling up a blunt. He stopped what he was doing when he saw us walking toward him. He stood from his seat, giving me a hug.

"Happy Birthday!" I said, hugging him back.

"Thank you," he said, sitting back down to finish rolling his blunt. "You are welcome to anything on the table, and if you want something different, just call a waitress over. Everything is on me tonight." I nodded my head even though I had no intentions of drinking tonight.

Looking around the VIP section, I noticed there were a lot of people in here. I counted at least ten dudes and a bunch of thirsty-looking females surrounding them. There were bottles of alcohol all over the place, and the familiar stench of weed floated in the air. It didn't take me long to realize that mostly everyone was either drunk or high. I grabbed a bottle of cranberry juice and poured it into a small plastic cup before I took a seat next to Tori. I watched on as I saw people on the dance floor dancing and having a good time. Normally, I hated being around crowds, but I pushed past my discomfort and tried to enjoy myself.

About an hour later, it seemed as if the crowd had grown even more. I found myself enjoying the atmosphere despite being alone. Tori had long ago left me when Justin told her he wanted to show her something after she gave him a lap dance. It didn't take a rocket scientist to know what they were probably doing right now.

"Hey, where are the restrooms?" I asked the waitress that was clearing the empty bottles off the table. Drinking all those cups of juice had my bladder full.

"It's down there to your left." She pointed in the direction. I thanked her before making my way through the dance floor. I got stopped several times by dudes asking me for a dance, but I politely declined.

I was so happy when I finally made it inside of the restroom. I ran to an empty stall, relieving my bladder. Once I was done handling my business, I refreshed my makeup and applied more gloss to my lips before walking out. I was on my way back to my section when I noticed people staring at something. I turned in the direction everyone was looking in, and my body stiffened when I spotted the last person I wanted to see.

People parted like the Red Sea as Ron glided through the crowd. You would've thought he was Jay-Z or somebody from the way people were calling out to him and women damn near rushing him to get his attention even though he was paying them no mind as he made his way into the VIP section I had just left from. Justin greeted him, pulling him into a brotherly hug. Another guy came over, and they shared a laugh together.

I couldn't lie; he was looking good as fuck in his all-black suit with his dreads hanging loosely around his face. He was definitely on his grown man shit tonight. I had to squeeze my legs tightly together to control my raging hormones, hating the fact that even his mere presence still had an effect on me. *I was going to kill Tori's lying ass*, I thought.

Looking back up in his is direction, I saw at least three women approaching him, and to my surprise, he was engaging with them. I half expected him to send them away. I felt a tinge of jealousy as I watched those women smile in his face. It was officially time for me to leave.

I was so busy thinking about my exit plan that I didn't realize someone was tapping me on the shoulder. Turning around, I saw Shawn standing behind me.

"What are you doing here?" I asked, pleasantly surprised. This wasn't usually his type of scene. Hell, it wasn't mine either

He moved closer to my ear so I could hear him over the loud music. "My cousin invited me, so I thought I would show my face for a while before I bounced. What about you?"

"Same thing. Do you remember my cousin Tori?"

He nodded his head. "How could I forget that crazy ass girl?" He laughed.

"Well, this is actually her boyfriend's party, so she dragged me along with her."

Just as I was about to ask him another question, "B.E.D." by Jacquees blasted through the speakers.

"Do you want to dance?"

I shook my head in protest. "You know I don't know how to dance."

"Just follow my lead." He grinned, pulling me to the dance floor. Our bodies swayed back and forth as the music continued to play. I looked around and saw people grinding on each other, making me wonder if that's what we were supposed to be doing. "You look beautiful," he whispered in my ear, causing me to blush.

"Thank you. And you don't look bad yourself," I complimented him back, resting my head on his chest. Though, I was happy to see him, I kept my eyes on the VIP section, wondering if Ron knew I was here, and if he did, would he care? It was funny how you could think you were over a person until you saw them again. I thought I was over him, but apparently, I wasn't. Once the song ended, I pulled myself away from his body.

"I'm about to leave up out of here. But I want to see you tomorrow. I have something that I want you to see."

"Well, I'm free all day, so just give me a call." We hugged, and he kissed me on the cheek before heading toward the exit.

I watched him disappear into the sea of people, wearing a smile on my face. Suddenly, I got this strange feeling like I was being watched. Surveying the room, I tried to find the person, but I couldn't. *Maybe I was imagining things.* I shrugged it off. I went back into our section to tell Tori I was leaving. I was starting to get sleepy, and the heels were killing my feet. My eyes scanned the room, trying to spot Ron, but there was no sign of him. A small part of me was hoping to catch one last glimpse of him before I left, but maybe it was for the best that I didn't see him.

I said my goodbyes and went out the door that I came in. As soon as I opened the door, I hugged my body tightly. It seemed like the temperature dropped even more. I ran to my car, trying to get out of this cold air. I froze when I saw Ron leaning his body against my car, taking a pull of the blunt he was smoking, then blowing the smoke out of his nose. I slowly approached him, wondering why he was by my car.

"Umm, I need to leave, so can you move?" I asked as nicely as I could. All the hurt that I felt from his rejection was slowly starting to surface again.

He turned his head in my direction, giving me a stoic look, taking another pull of his blunt before answering me. "Did you let that nigga fuck?" he questioned. I already knew he was referring to Shawn.

I jerked my head back, not believing he had the nerve to ask me that shit. We hadn't spoken to each other in over a month, and that's the first thing to came out his mouth? I wanted to slap the shit out of him just for asking me that. "I don't think that's any of your business. Last time I checked, I was a single woman that could do what the fuck I wanted to do," I spat, placing my hands over my chest.

He chuckled to himself before stepping on his blunt. Next thing I knew, he was standing in my personal space, giving me a cold stare. "I guess that nigga got you smelling yourself—because clearly, you forgot who the fuck you are talking to. Now answer my goddamn question. Did you give my pussy away to that nigga?" he spoke with venom in his voice.

I wanted to be a smart ass, but I quickly decided against it once I saw the menacing look in his eyes. I might have been mad at him, but I wasn't crazy enough to try him like that. So I did the next best thing I could think of. I remained silent.

"You think I'm playing with yo' ass, huh?" He pulled out his phone, dialing a number. "Aye, do you remember that nigga that I pointed out to you? Find out where he lay his head at and get back to me," he said, ending the call, stuffing his phone in his pocket. "Since you want to be on mute and shit, I guess I'll have to ask the nigga myself, and if he tells me some shit that I don't want to hear, you might need to get a funeral outfit ready."

My eyes widened with fear. If I didn't know he was crazy before, I knew it now. "Are you serious, right now!" I yelled at him. Even though I was cold a minute ago, my body temperature began to rise with anger building up inside me. "How dare you try to control me by threatening to do something to my friend. To answer your stupid ass question, no, I'm not fucking him. You don't want me, remember? So why should it matter to you who I'm seeing? You need to worry less about what I'm doing and more about those other hoes that you are fucking," I said, trying to push past him.

The next thing I knew, Ron picked me up and slung me over his shoulder, carrying me away from my car. I started yelling and screaming for him to put me down. But it fell on deaf ears. There were a few partygoers who looked in our direction to see what was going on, but once they saw who it was, they went on about their business.

He pulled out his keys to his black Phantom, and I heard his car alarm chirp. He opened the passenger door and threw me in and closed the door. I tried to get out, but it wouldn't open. *I knew this nigga didn't just put a child lock on this door,* I thought, pulling at the door handle. He climbed in the car, pulling off.

"Turn back around and take me to my damn car. I don't want to be around you. What about that don't you understand?" I asked through gritted teeth. The truth of the matter was I didn't want to be around him, because I was scared of what might happen.

"Well, that's too fucking bad." He stared at the road.

"I can't stand yo' ass! You make me so damn sick! We have been doing a good job of avoiding each other, so why, all of a sudden, you want to be around me, questioning if I'm having sex with someone else? You haven't spoken to me in over a month, but I see you driving past my apartment every other week, going to fuck someone else! You don't give a damn about me! You said you didn't want me, but it's a problem when I move on? Just let me out of this car!" I screamed, crying tears of frustration.

"Sit yo' ass back, buckle your seat belt, and shut the fuck up," he said, completely dismissing me.

I huffed as I leaned back in my seat with an angry pout on my face, wiping away my tears. There wasn't much I could do at this point anyways. It wasn't like I could escape, and my phone had died, so I couldn't call anyone. The only thing left for me to do was see how this night would play out. "Could you at least turn up the heat? That's the least you could do since I'm basically being kidnapped," I sarcastically said to him.

He did as I asked, and we rode in silence for close to thirty minutes. I took this time to look up through the roof of the car and admire the stars as they gave light to the dark sky. Even though it was cold, it was a beautiful night. I felt the car slowing down, causing me to look out the window. I frowned in confusion when I noticed we were sitting in front of a construction site. From what I could tell, it looked as if someone was having a mansion built.

"What are we doing here?"

"This is my house that I'm having built from the ground up. I come here sometimes to look at the process that's being made and when I have a lot of shit on my mind and want to be left alone. You are the first person to see this," he responded, still staring out the windshield.

"My mama told me you came to visit me while I was in the hospital. Why did you come?" He finally looked in my direction, giving me an intense stare.

"I don't know. I guess out of concern," I replied, playing with my thumbs, not wanting to give him the real reason.

"Concern, huh?" He chuckled, giving me a knowing look. "Aight, ma. If that's the excuse you want to use. You look beautiful tonight. Straight hair looks good on you even though I prefer your natural hair."

I was taken aback by his sudden change of attitude. Less than an hour ago, he had held me hostage, cursed me out, and threatened me, but now he was giving me a compliment. I didn't know how to take it, so I just gave him the side eye. "Thank you," I replied slowly. More silence adorned us. "How have you've been doing since the accident?" I figured since he was trying to act civil, so would I.

"I'm straight. I just can't sleep on my left side for right now because of the stitches." I nodded my head. "I don't know what you said to my mama, but she has been getting on my nerves, trying to get information out me about you."

"Really? I didn't say anything. She just asked me how I knew you, and that was about it."

"Do you think you have what it takes to be my ride or die?" he asked in a serious tone.

"What?" He had caught me off guard with that question.

He continued. "I'm a complicated ass nigga. It takes a lot to deal with someone like me. I know how to make money and provide—that comes easy to me—but I don't know shit about dating or being in a relationship. I have a short temper, and any little thing can set me off, and I'm moody as fuck. I like having my own space. I'm not the most understanding ass nigga either. I don't deal well with emotions, and if I'm being honest, I could give a damn about all that love shit. But when it comes to you, I feel something different. I don't know what the fuck that feeling is, but it's there, and it won't go away. I ain't never been the one to catch feelings. I'm used to fucking and going as I please with no strings attached. That's how I've been living my life since I started fucking. All this shit is new to me." His hazel eyes were staring into mines. If I weren't mistaken, it seemed like he was a little nervous and unsure of himself.

"So you saying all this to say what exactly?" I asked, trying to figure out the direction of the conversation.

He reached over and softly stroked the side of my face. "I'm willing to give this whole relationship shit a try with you. It's gon' be times where I fuck up, but you have to remember all this shit is gon' be new to me. I'mma be out of town for a couple of days, and while I'm gone, I want you to think about what I just told you. I'll hit you up when I come back, and you can give me an answer then."

I sat there in my seat, speechless, thinking over everything he'd just confessed to me. He was telling me something that I wanted to hear for over a month, but could I really handle him and the things that came along with being with him? And what about Shawn? He had been there for me since he came back into my life, and I did start to develop feelings for him, but they weren't as strong as the ones I had for Ron.

On paper, Shawn would definitely be the better choice, but my heart was pulling me more toward Ron. We had a connection between us that couldn't be explained. I didn't want to hurt Shawn, but I also didn't want to choose him out of pity either. I really had to think on it before I made any drastic decisions.

"Okay," I respond in a soft voice. "What made you change your mind?" I wanted to know.

He gave me a sexy smirk before gently pinching my jaw. "You'll find that out when you give me your answer. Come on so I can show you around."

I looked at him like he was crazy. "It's freezing out there, and I'm not trying to catch a cold."

He pulled off the jacket he was wearing and passed it to me. I quickly put it on as he unlocked the door. I inhaled the scent of the jacket and melted. It smelled just like the cologne I'd grown to love him wearing.

Once I stepped out the car, he grabbed my hand with his left and turned on a flashlight with his right. We circled around the place as he told me what he planned to have, and which floor would have what on it. I looked at him as he explained everything. He looked so passionate about building his home that I couldn't help but admire him even more. I loved being around this version of him versus the angry one, but I knew that if I did choose him, I would have to except that part as well.

The ride back to my car was a quiet one, which I appreciated because I didn't know what to say to him after what he told me. Once

DANIELLE MAY

we made it back to the club, I was surprised to see people still standing outside. I would've thought the party had been ended.

Ron pulled up beside my car, and I tried to open the door. "You have to unlock the door so I can get out."

He pressed a button on the side of his door, and the latch instantly went up. I went to open the door but stopped when I felt Ron pulling me back, roughly planting a kiss on my lips. My body reacted to his touch as I felt a familiar spark run down my spine as I allowed him to explore my month with his tongue. Placing both of my hands on the side of his face, I kissed him back with even more intensity.

I felt his strong hands caressing my thighs, slowly making their way up to my vagina that was soaking wet. He pushed my panties to the side then slid a finger inside of my secret spot, causing me to let out a soft moan. We continued to kiss as he fingered me. Feeling an orgasm approaching, I started throwing my pussy back on his finger. I was almost there when, suddenly, he slid his finger from inside of me.

I opened my eyes in confusion. "Why did you stop?" I whined.

He chuckled. "I was checking to make sure you wasn't lying to me. From the way that pussy was gripping my finger, I got my answer. Now get yo' horny ass out my damn car, fucking up my seat," he said, dismissing me.

If looks could've killed, he would've been six feet under. I glared at him one last time before getting out the car and purposely slamming the door. I thought that would get a reaction out of him, but it didn't. He just sped off.

Asshole.

45

****

Bobbing my head to the sounds of J. Cole's voice blaring through my headphones, I worked on a nature-themed painting for a new customer that had seen some of my work on Instagram, thanks to Tori. Lately, things had been picking up for me in my professional life. No, I wasn't making any progress with finding a paint dealer, but I had gotten several new customers. I wasn't exactly where I wanted to be, but it was a start.

Now, my personal life, on the other hand, was giving me a headache. I still couldn't make a decision on whom I really wanted to be with. For most people, it would be a no-brainer, but to me, it wasn't that simple. On one hand, I had Shawn, a person whom I'd been friends with since the age of sixteen. He was sweet, caring, and successful, and I had no doubt in my mind that he would make a great husband and father one day. Then, on the other hand, I had Ron, an unapologetic, egotistical, asshole that needed anger management but somehow made me feel things I never felt every time I was near him. It could be the fact that he was my first that had me feeling this way, but I thought there was more to it than that.

The ringing of my phone invaded my ear through my headphones. I set my painting board on the dresser, answering the phone.

"Hey," I answered.

"Open the door, I have something to show you," Shawn said before hanging up.

Walking down the hallway, I used the towel on my shoulder to wipe off the extra paint that was on my hands before opening the door for him.

He rushed past me with a laptop in his hands, taking a seat on my sofa. I watched curiously as he opened the laptop and pulled up a page. He patted the space beside him with a huge grin on his face. "Are you just going to stand there or come over here to see what I have to show you?"

I made my way over, taking the seat beside him, looking at the screen. I wasn't exactly sure what I was supposed to be looking at. There were a bunch of different tabs pulled up. I guess he could see that I was confused because he pointed to the one he wanted me to see. "Click on it," he eagerly said.

I did as I was told, clicking on the tab he pointed to. I gasped in shock once I saw what it was. It was an art site that had a big picture of me, surrounded by smaller pictures of my paintings. I looked over at him for an explanation. "What's this about?"

"Well," he started off. "I know that you are struggling to get your work out there, so I thought maybe I could help you out a little. I do have a successful website business, so why not use it to promote your work?"

"How did you even get these pictures?" I whispered, scrolling down the screen, still in shock of what I was seeing.

"When I was here a few weeks ago, I took a few pictures of them while you were using the bathroom. I had to be quick, though, because you pee fast as hell," he teased me with a smile.

"Thank you," I said with tears in my eyes, truly grateful for the gift he gave me. I leaped on Shawn with my arms wide open, giving him a hug that caused him to fall back on the sofa. This might not have been a big deal for him, but it meant so much to me. When I vented to him about my frustration of not being where I wanted to be at, I would've never guessed that he would take in everything that I had told him and do this. "You have no idea how much this means to me."

I felt his arms wrap around my body, returning the hug. "I'm just glad I could help."

I slowly pulled away from him, sniffing my nose and wiping my eyes. "Well, you still didn't have to do it, and just for that, you have earned yourself a meal personally cooked by me." Walking to the kitchen, I opened the refrigerator to see what all I had. "What are you in the mood for?" I called out to him.

"I'mma have to take a rain check. I have to make a couple of runs. I just stopped by to show you the website," he replied, entering the kitchen.

"You have been running a lot of errands lately. What exactly do these *errands* consist of you doing?" I inquired, turning around to face him.

"Just business stuff," he nonchalantly said back. Something was telling me that there was more to the story, but I didn't want to pressure him into telling me. If he wanted me to know, then he'd tell me eventually. He glanced down at his watch. "I got to get going." He walked back into the living room, grabbing his things. I followed behind him to the door. "When can I expect an answer from you?"

"Soon," I assured him.

"Aight, I'll be waiting to finally treat you like the queen that you are."

"What exactly is the role of a queen?" When it came to the term 'queen,' I didn't see it as a term of endearment.

"A queen is a woman that, even when a man may be flawed and broken at times, builds him up and helps him become the king he needs to be. I'm a king that needs a strong queen—a queen that is strong willed, intelligent, and doesn't need me but appreciates me. One who will check me when I get outta pocket and can also accept correction when she is wildin'. Someone I can trust to be there when I need her 'cause I'll always be there. Someone that we can grow together, and goes without saying, she is beautiful," he said, winking at me.

"But the queen has no real voice. She is expected to be everything to a king, but what does he do for her? Where will she go if she don't have enough energy to give him anything?" I challenged.

"My queen's voice will always, always be heard and respected. Just like she is expected to be everything to me, I also will be everything to her. I will always do whatever I can to make her feel appreciated and valued. If she has no energy to give, then I'll do my part to give to help her back up. If she's with me when I'm down, what kind of king would I be? What kind of man that would make me? That's what children do. When things get difficult, he just can't run—can't just freeze." He walked up to me. "And that's good for her because I never freeze." He gave me a quick peck on the lips before making his way down the steps. "I'll holla at you later."

Just as he was walking down the stairs, I noticed Tori walking up, stopping him. "Oh, damn, you are fine. I thought Sasha was over exaggerating when she said you resembled Kofi Siriboe sexy ass." She put her index finger between her teeth, lustfully taking him in. "You better be lucky I'm a faithful ass bitch, or I would gladly tie your ass up and give you this work."

"Thank you, I think." He blushed with embarrassment. I could tell from his sudden change in demeanor that he was a little bit uncomfortable with her boldness toward him.

"If you don't bring yo' crazy butt up these stairs and leave that man alone," I called out through clenched teeth, trying to save Shawn from her.

She made her way up the stairs. "What?" she asked innocently. "I was just admiring God's work. It ain't my fault that he look delicious enough to eat—well, suck in this case." I closed the door behind us, ignoring her foolishness.

"What do I owe the pleasure of this visit?" I asked sarcastically, grabbing my juice off the coffee table.

"The better question is what was you doing up in here with that sexy ass man that just left? I see you wearing them short ass shorts, exposing those lil' cheeks of yours." She pinched my ass before sitting in the same spot Shawn just left. "You ain't fooling nobody."

I waved her comment off. "Nobody was up in here doing anything. He legit only stayed for less than ten minutes. So you can get your nasty ass mind out the gutter."

"Girl, I can't help but think nasty. I'm going through withdrawal. Justin has been gone for three days—a whole three days. I'm feenin' for his dick right now," she whined, throwing her head back on the couch pillow.

"There is always FaceTime sex," I offered a suggestion.

She shot up her head and frowned up her face like I had disrespected her. "That don't do nothing for me but piss me the fuck off. That's like wanting a steak but settling for chicken instead."

"I don't know what to tell you then," I said, giggling at her expense.

"Oh, you think this is funny? I can't wait until you start getting dicked down on a regular basis so you can feel my pain."

"No offense, but if it makes me act anything like you, I don't want to experience it."

"Girl, whatever." She rolled her eyes. "Anyways, I need a favor."

"What's up?"

She smiled, clasping her hands together. "Justin and I anniversary is next month, so I thought it would be cute or whatever if you could paint a big ass portrait of us. This picture." She pulled out her phone and showed me the picture. "Of course, I'm getting him something else to go along with it, but yeah, this will be my gift."

Nodding my head, I agreed. "Just send the picture to my phone, and I'll start on it as soon as I can."

"Thank you!" she screamed excitedly. "And just so you know, I will be paying you, and I don't want to hear a damn thing about it."

I wanted to protest, but I figured it would be no use. "Can I ask you something? Y'all been together for seven, going on eight, years. Have you ever thought about getting married?"

She gave me a thoughtful look before answering. "Honestly, I really haven't. I mean, yes, it crossed my mind a time or two, but I just don't obsess over it. In my mind, we are already married. The only thing we don't have is a legal document stating that we are. We live together, and he pays the bills, allowing me to save my money. We fuss, fight, make up, and we have a good communication system going on."

"So you don't see yourself being *legally* married anytime soon?"

"I'll put it like this. If it happens, it happens; if it doesn't, I won't be tripping over it, but enough about this marriage shit. What do you have to eat? I'm starving right now. I haven't eaten all day," she said, dramatically caressing her stomach.

"It's some wings in there, but you have to cook them."

She got up from her seat. "Damn, yo' ass really need to learn how to cook. Do you have any buffalo sauce? I want to make some hot wings."

"Yeah, I just bought some. Check in the cabinet on the left side of the stove!" I yelled, walking back down the hallway. "I need to finish up this painting before tomorrow. Come and get me when the food is ready." Trying to get back in the zone, I put the headphones back in my ear, resuming my music as I picked up my tools, painting away.

Ron

Twirling a loose dread between my fingers, I stared out the window on the jet, seeing the runway up ahead. We had just gotten back in town from a business trip to Cuba, and I was glad as fuck. The whole trip irked my fucking nerves to the maximum. I didn't like for my time to be wasted, and that's exactly what this trip was—a waste of fucking time.

This new connect that Justin's father introduced us to thought we were some lil' niggas that he could punk, trying to sell us some product that wasn't worth the amount that he was asking for. Then, Bryan's stupid ass thought it would be a good idea to run off with two random bitches he had just met and ended up getting robbed by them, leaving him stranded in the middle of nowhere, ass naked. Justin and I had to get out our bed in the middle of the fucking night to save his ass. When we pulled up on him, he had a bunch of leaves covering his dick and ass. Even though that shit was funny, I was still pissed off at him.

Bryan turned around in his seat, facing us with a serious expression on his face. "Aye, real quick before we leave off this plane, y'all niggas better not say shit about what happened to me. I have a reputation to keep."

Justin and I both looked at each other before looking back at him. "You don't have to worry about us telling no damn body how yo' ass was in the middle of the road, ass naked, looking like a fucked up version of Tarzan. We'll get clowned on by association." He laughed before texting away on his phone.

"Fuck you," he spat, turning around in his seat.

"Get out your fucking feelings and stop acting like a bitch," Justin said, throwing a ball of paper at him, which he threw it back. I just shook my head at these immature niggas.

Once we landed and collected our shit, we went to our cars that were parked beside each other.

"What are you about to get into?" Justin asked me, putting his things in the truck before closing it shut.

I scratched my scalp, making me realize that it was time to go get my dreads washed and re-twisted. "About to pull up on my parents and see what they are talking about before I head home."

"Cool. We still meeting up later on tonight to discuss how we are going to go about finding another connect?"

"Nawl, we can do that shit tomorrow. I'm tired as fuck, and I know when I go home, I'm not gon' feel like leaving out of that bitch."

He nodded his head. "Aight, be easy, my nigga." We dapped each other up before getting in our cars, speeding off.

On the drive to my parents' home, I had a lot of shit on my mind. This trip experience had me thinking about retiring earlier than I initially planned. I was getting too old to be dealing with the unnecessary shit that came along with being in this drug game. I had better things to do with my time than to be arguing with motherfuckers about shit that I was trying to buy off their hands and make them some money. That's like begging a store to let you shop there. I'd rather just pull the fuck out now before I ended up killing one of those motherfuckers and ending up having a bigger issue on my hand.

My thoughts switched over to Sasha. I didn't know what the fuck that girl did to me, but she had me feeling emotions that I didn't even know I had. She had me thinking about being on some exclusive type shit with her. Even though I was still fucking around with some bad ass bitches, they didn't have shit on her.

The first time we had sex, that shit was amazing. She had me biting my lips to keep from moaning and shit. I bit down so hard on them that I drew blood. I surprised my own damn self when I let the word 'shit' escape my lips because I never said shit during sex. It wasn't like she was doing any extra-freaky type shit either.

If I was being perfectly honest, compared to the bitches that I was used to fucking, her sex game was average at best, but I didn't hold it against her, seeing as how I was her first and all. But the difference between her sex and the other hoes was when I fucked them, that's the only thing it was. Fucking. When I fucked Sasha, I felt like I had a connection with her. I knew I had a fucked up way of showing it, but I really did have a soft spot for her stuck-up ass, and I was willing to explore it.

Deciding to hit her up, I pulled out my phone to dial her number. It went straight to voicemail, so I assumed that she had put her phone on airplane mode. It wasn't out of the ordinary for her to do that when she didn't want anyone interrupting her while she was in, in her words, her 'creative zone.' I made a mental note to pop up on her ass after I left from my parents.

Pulling up at a red light, I waited impatiently for it to turn green. I surveyed the area, watching people walk on the sidewalk. There weren't many people around, because of this cold ass weather—just a hand full. Then something caught my attention.

"What the fuck?" I had to do a double take when I saw Sasha across the street, walking with that nigga that she was dancing with that night at the club. As soon as the light turned green, I busted a U-turn and parked my car on the other side of the sidewalk. I didn't give a shit about looking both ways before crossing the street. I had one thing on my mind, and that was finding out why the fuck she was with this nigga.

They were so busy grinning and shit that they didn't see me walking up on them. "What the fuck so damn funny that got you laughing and shit? I want to laugh too," I said, making my presence known, startling them.

When they turned around, Sasha looked as if she saw a damn ghost but said nothing, and the nigga wore a confused look on his face like he didn't know what was going on. Sizing him up, he was an inch or two shorter than me, and his muscle was damn near nonexistent. It didn't take me long to realize that he was one of those square ass niggas.

"I asked you a question," I spoke again, glaring at her.

"Ron, this is my friend, Shawn. Shawn, this is Ron," she introduced us. He reached out his hand so I could take it, but I just looked at that bitch like it was infected.

"Okay," he mumbled, lowering his hand.

"Do you always have to be so damn rude to people?" She huffed, peering at me with an attitude, but I didn't give a fuck. I had some question for their asses.

Looking over in the lame nigga's direction, I asked, "Have you fucked her?" I pointed toward Sasha. "Have you looked at the pussy? Have you smelled the pussy? Have you touched the pussy?"

"Are you fucking serious right now? You are being childish," she spat, but I ignored her, awaiting his answer. I hoped for his stake that all of the answers to my questions were a no, or this would be his last day breathing.

"I don't think that that's any of your business. You don't know me well enough to ask me no shit like that, and you are being disrespectful to Sasha," he said, giving me a hard look.

Momentarily looking away, I chuckled to myself, something that I did when I was about to blow up. I turned my attention back in his direction, approaching him. We were standing inches from each other. "Look, nigga, I tried asking yo' ass nicely what you have going on with Sasha, but since yo' Black ass want to grow a pair of nuts and come at me sideways, then I'mma put it like this. Answer my fucking question or get yo' ass beat out here in these streets."

Sasha tried to step in between us. I guess it was her way of trying to diffuse the situation. "Please don't do this. People are watching us," she begged, looking around at the audience we had acquired. I didn't give a damn if someone called the police. Shit, I knew most of them

niggas personally anyways.

"Like I told you before, that's none of your damn business what we have going on, so if that's the only thing that you came over here for, then you can walk back where you came from because you ain't scaring shit over here, my nigga."

I gently pushed Sasha's body to the side, and before she could stop anything, my fist had connected with his jaw, causing him to stumble a little. He called himself trying to run up on me, but I caught him with a right hook. We were in a full-fledged fight at this point. I could hear Sasha screaming for us to stop, but I wasn't listening. The only thing on my mind was beating this nigga's ass.

He punched me in the stomach, hitting my side that hadn't fully healed, causing me to hiss in pain. When he did that, I saw red. I started going in on him with all the energy I had until I felt like he deserved enough. There was blood running from his nose, and I had busted his lips. I stood over his body as he tried to get up, and I kicked him one more time in the side before moving away from him.

Sasha was crying, trying to walk over to him and help him up, but I quickly deadened that shit. "Where the fuck you think you are going?" I asked, grabbing her by the arm. She tried jerking away, but my grip was too strong for her.

"I'm going to see if Shawn is okay," she said, still trying to pull away from me to get to him.

That just made me even more pissed off.

"No the fuck you not!" I shouted in her face. "What you are about to do is tell this fuck ass nigga that you are my bitch now! Then you are going to walk yo' ass on the other side of the street to my car and get in!"

She brushed her tears away, glaring at me angrily. "I'm not about to do sh—"

Before she could finish whatever the fuck she was about to say, I picked her little ass up and threw her over my shoulder, carrying her to my car.

I stopped then looked back at him one last time. "This is your first and last warning. Stay away from my bitch."

I hoped I made myself crystal clear. I'd be the first to admit that I was selfish. Now that I had claimed her, I wasn't about to share her with any-damn-body.

Once I threw her little ass in the car, I pulled off, en route to my parents'. I figured since I cared about her enough to put a title on what we had, I might as well let her meet them. Granted, it could've been under better circumstances, but that was her damn fault.

"Pull this fucking car over now! I have to make sure Shawn is okay!" she frantically cried, beating on my dashboard like she lost her damn mind. For her to be acting this way over that nigga let me know that it was more than some friendly shit going on between them.

I slammed down on the brakes hard in the middle of the road. The cars behind me were honking their horns, yelling out the windows. I rolled down the window, sticking my middle finger up so they could see. When they saw that I wasn't moving, they got into the other lane, driving off.

"What is the fuck wrong with you, beating on my shit like you don't have any fucking sense! What the fuck you and this nigga really got going on for you to be this damn worried over him?" I questioned.

"Just take me back, please. I want to know if he is fine. Plus, my cellphone is in his car." She still had tears rolling down her face as she spoke in a whispered tone.

I didn't know what made me more pissed off. The fact that she felt comfortable riding in the car with this nigga or the fact she was sitting in my face and crying over him.

"I'm telling you now that shit ain't happening. So you might as well wipe them tears away and enjoy this damn ride," I said, resuming driving.

"I fucking hate you. I really want you to know that." She glared at me. "I can't believe I would even associate myself with someone like you. And here I am again in another messed up situation," she said more to herself than me.

"If you think you are 'bout to try and distance yourself away from me again, I'm telling you now, it's not going to work out how you think it will. Now that I gave you the title as being my bitch, you ain't going nowhere until I get tired of being around yo' ass or if you be on some trifling, hoe shit."

"Last time I checked, I didn't open my mouth and agree to be with your psycho ass. And seeing the way you carried on back there didn't help your case at all. It made it worse. So I'm good on you." She tried to play tough, but I could see straight through her fake ass act. Sure, she was mad at my ass right now, but she wasn't done fucking with me—not by a long shot.

"You can keep telling yourself that lie, but we both know the truth."

I reached my hand over, cuffing one of her breasts with a little bit of force but not enough to cause any pain. When I heard her yell ouch and hit me with that soft ass lick, I grinned a little. "You know you like that," I said, attempting to grab it again, but she inched away from my arm, moving her body closer to the door.

"I don't like anything about you right now. Matter of fact, the only words I want to hear come out of your mouth is you saying that you are about to take me home. Other than that, don't say shit to me, and I definitely won't say shit to you." She leaned her head back against the seat, looking out of the window with attitude written all over her face.

I started to say something to her smart-mouthed ass, but I didn't pay her any attention. She wouldn't be screaming that 'don't say nothing to me shit' when she saw where I was taking her. She was gon' be begging me for conversation. So I turned up my music as loud as it could go because I knew she hated loud music booming in her ears, and I continued driving.

I saw her in my peripheral, giving me the death stare, but I ignored her. Normally, I didn't do all this petty shit, because I felt like we were too grown to be doing this childish shit, and I didn't have time for it. But since she wanted to act stupid, I was going to act stupid right along with her.

Pulling up to the gate of my parents' crib, I keyed in the code, watching the gates open. Parking in my usual spot, I cut off the engine. I turned my head toward Sasha as I saw her mouth slightly gap open and her eyes widen in amazement. I expected this reaction from her. That shit never failed. Everyone that saw their house for the first time always did that.

"Are you just going to sit there like a deer caught in headlights, or are you going to get out of the car?" I asked, already opening the door.

"Is this your house?" she inquired, still memorized.

"Nawl, this is my parents' crib, so get yo' little ass out so you can meet them."

"What!" she screamed in my ear, damn near bursting my eardrum. "Why would you bring me here? I can't meet them. Look at how I'm dressed." She panicked, motioning up and down her body with her hands.

My eyes traveled down her body, surveying what she was wearing. She had on a pair of green tights or leggings, whichever the fuck they were, a long, white, plain shirt that fit a little loose on her frame with a pink bomber on top of it, and a pair of pink UGG boots. Her hair was in a ponytail on top of her head with a few loose strands out. Even though she looked basic with what she had on, she was still pretty as fuck.

"Ain't shit wrong with what you got on," I said, stepping out the car and closing the door behind me. I started making my way toward the door when I realized that she was still in the car, biting her nails, looking all scared and shit. I approached the side of her door, opening it before leaning up against it. "What the fuck you waiting for? Get out the car."

She looked at the house again before looking back at me, wearing a worried expression. "You can go in there by yourself. I'll just wait out here until you are done doing whatever it is that you came here to do."

"Why are you making it seem like I took you to a haunted house or some shit? You are just going to meet two regular people that just so happen to be my parents. You met my mother, and they already know that you are here anyways. It's cameras at the gate entrance. So stop acting childish, act yo' damn age, and get out this car."

She just sat there, not even making an attempt to move. This shit was getting fucking ridiculous. "Get out the fucking car now, Sasha," I demanded, slowly starting to lose the little patience that I had with her. Still, she sat there like a statue. Since she wanted to play, I had something for that ass.

I leaned my tall frame inside the car, reaching over her body to unfasten the seatbelt. I used one of my arms to place behind her back and the other under her legs, picking her up bridal style. I used my leg to kick the door shut. She kicked and squirmed, trying to escape, but it was no use. I was too strong. When we were close to the door, my mom's face appeared, and she opened it.

"What are you doing, Ron? Put that girl down. She can walk by herself," she scolded, allowing us to enter. Loosening my hold, I slowly released her, making sure her feet were planted on the floor before I let go of her. She tried smoothing down her clothes, glaring at me in the process.

My mother walked over to Sasha, giving her a motherly hug. "I told you I would be seeing you again." She released her. Sasha gave her an uneasy smile, still nervous.

"So I don't get no love? That's so messed up." I playfully pretended to be hurt as I nodded my head. "I'mma remember that when you want something for Christmas. You know it's only a few months away."

She smacked me upside the head before pulling me into a hug then letting go. "That was for all that cussing you were doing outside."

"Where is Dad?" I questioned, following behind her to the kitchen. I didn't know what she was cooking, but it smelled good as hell. My stomach started to growl a little, reminding me that I hadn't eaten shit since we left from Cuba.

"He is in his office on a business call," she answered, checking on whatever it was in the stove before closing it back and giving me her attention. "He is probably done now. You should go in there and check."

"Bet. But before I go, I want to officially introduce y'all. Sasha, this is my mama. Ma, this is my new, irritating girlfriend, Sasha. We just made it official before we got here. So do that interrogating shit that a mother is supposed to do and let me know what you think. And don't go soft on her petty ass either." I ran out the room, trying to dodge whatever item I was sure my mother was going to throw at me for cursing in front of her. Seconds later, I saw a fork flying at me, missing my body only by a couple of inches.

"I'm going to beat your ass when you come back in here!" she yelled.

"You'll have to catch me first, old lady!"

Laughing, I made my way to my dad's office that was located on the other side of the house. I opened the door, not caring enough to knock. He was seated behind his desk in his brown chair with his cellphone pressed against his ear. When he saw that I was standing there, he lifted his index finger, telling me to give him a minute, and pointed toward the chair that was in front of him. I took a seat, sliding down in my chair a little, trying to get comfortable. I looked around at all the paintings he had decorating his wall. There was a number of pictures, but each looked like it told a different story. It was funny how I didn't care about none of this art shit until I started fucking with Sasha.

"What can I do for you?" my dad spoke, ending his call, setting his phone on top of his desk, and giving me his full attention.

"I came to talk to you about that crooked ass connect Uncle Mo tried to put us on," I said, clenching my jaw, getting mad just thinking about it. Unlike my mother, my dad didn't give a fuck about my cussing in front of him.

He leaned back in his chair. "Yeah, I heard about what happened. No, I don't agree with how Mo had y'all going on a dummy mission. Between you and me, he has never been the brains of our operation. I agree with the way that you handled yourself. I would've did the same shit as well. My next question is, what are your plans moving forward?"

I let out a deep sigh, running my hands over my dreads. "Honestly, I don't know. I've been giving some thought into retiring. I'm not built to be dealing with shit like this anymore. I'm in a whole other headspace," I confessed. I wanted to see how he felt about my revelation. Don't get me wrong; I was going to do what I wanted to do regardless of whether he approved of it or not.

He nodded his head. "If that's the move that you think you should make, then do it. I never intended for you to be involved in this type of life. I wanted you to go to college and have a couple of degrees under your belt, which you did. It just so happened that even though you had all these things going for yourself, you followed in my footsteps. I never quite understood your decision behind that, but I didn't question it either."

I thought back to the day that I told him I wanted to be part of his drug business when I was eighteen. I had always been a forward-thinking person, and I knew I couldn't live off their money forever, and I damn sho' wasn't about to be slaving at a minimum-wage-paying job. Working for my dad would be the next best thing, and it turned out to be a good decision. I made a little over three thousand a week, and I was still able to go to school full time.

It wasn't until I graduated with my first degree that he offered me the position to take his place. After thinking it over, I took it. Justin and Bryan came, taking over their fathers' positions as well. Ever since then, we had been making money together with no plans of it slowing down. But I always told myself that when I neared the age of thirty, I would leave. Plus, I knew that Bryan and Justin were capable of running shit without me.

"Maybe it will finally make that mother of yours calm her nerves and stop talking my ear off about being worried about you and shit." He removed two glass cups from in his desk and set them on the table. Getting up from his seat, he went to retrieve the bottle of Scotch he had in his liquor cabinet. He returned to his seat and poured both of us a glass.

I took a sip, ignoring the burning sensation that occurred in my chest when I swallowed. "I don't think that woman will ever stopped worrying about me."

"I guess you are right about that. Maybe I should put a baby in her ass. They'll probably make her sit down somewhere," he thoughtfully said.

Nearly choking on my drink, I frowned my face in disgust. I knew this nigga really wasn't considering having a baby, and if that were the case, I didn't want to hear that shit. "I'll tell you like I told her. Y'all old asses better get a fucking dog or cat and call it a fucking day. Y'all should've got all that baby fever shit out of y'all system before passing the age of forty."

Laughing, he waved me off. "So who is the young lady I saw you carrying outside a couple of minutes ago?" He nodded his head toward the cameras behind him.

"This lil' shawty I'm fucking with heavy," I simply responded.

"You never brought a girl here before, so she must mean a great deal to you." He smirked, taking a sip of his drink.

"Yeah, som' like that." Though I brought her with me to meet them, I really didn't want to discuss her. I was new to this feelings shit, so it would take some time for me to be open about how I really felt about her. Shit, I had a hard enough time trying to figure that shit out myself, let alone to anyone else, especially her. One thing was for sure; I knew I liked her annoying ass.

He gave me a knowing look. "I know that look from anywhere.

Just a word of advice. Be prepared to take her feelings into consideration on a daily basis and say everything is your fault. You'll thank me later," he said, finishing off his drink, getting up from his seat. "Now let me go meet this young woman."

I gulped down the rest of my drink before getting up as well. "Where did you purchase all these paintings from?" I asked, stopping him before he could walk out the door.

"An old friend of mine is a famous art dealer, and he gives them to me for a discount." He gazed around the room at his pieces.

The wheels started turning in my head. I thought back on the conversations that I had with Sasha and her telling me about her dreams and aspirations. I knew she was having a hard time getting buyers for her painting, and this could possibly be her chance at a big break.

"Can you hook up a meeting between me and him?"

He gave me a curious stare. "I think that can be arranged. Why do you want to meet with him? Are you suddenly into art now?" he jokingly asked, walking out the door.

"Nawl, it ain't no shit like that. I got this person that paint, and the stuff is dope as hell. I'm sure once he lays eyes on it, he'll fuck with it," I spoke confidently. There wasn't a doubt in my mind that she was going to make it big. With the amount of talent she had, it was destined for her.

"Alright, I'mma take your word for it. I'll make the call later on tonight and text you the details."

We entered the kitchen. My mom and Sasha were sitting at the table, laughing about some shit, snacking on a plate of white chocolate strawberries. I was happy to see that she was no longer nervous and finally relaxed. Fucking with a nigga like me, that shy shit had to go. I didn't want a female like that. I needed one that commanded attention and didn't shy away from it.

"What's going on in here?" my dad spoke, startling the both of them, causing them to jump a little. He walked over toward my mom and leaned down to kiss her on the forehead. Sasha looked my way, rolling her eyes before taking another bite of her strawberry. That little attitude she had toward me was cute for the moment, but before she left out this bitch, it better be gone. I wouldn't hesitate to leave her stubborn ass here. I was sure my parents wouldn't have a problem taking her home since they were being all buddy-buddy now. "Hey, how you doing? My name is Kevin, and you are?"

She reached out her hand. "Oh, I'm sorry. I'm Sasha," she responded, wearing an innocent smile. Ain't this about some shit? I walked in here, and her ass was rolling her eyes at me, but when my dad said something to her, she was all smiles.

"It's a pleasure meeting you, Sasha. You are the first girl this knucklehead has ever invited over here, so I'm expecting to see more of you in the future. Just do me one favor, and make sure you keep him in line. His mouth tends to get him in a lot of trouble, which makes him hard to deal with." He smiled warmly.

"You don't got to tell me. I already know," she mumbled under her breath before smiling again, thinking that nobody heard that slick ass comment she made.

Walking past her to get something to drink out of the refrigerator, being an asshole, I purposely kicked her chair, causing her to drop the strawberry out of her mouth. She turned toward me, and I threw a smirk at her.

We stayed there longer than I intended. Once we all ate dinner, I tried leaving, but my mom found a way to keep us there. If she wasn't bringing up embarrassing ass stories about me, she was showing Sasha something. Eventually, I just said fuck it and went in the pool house to smoke my blunt. I wasn't worried about my mom tripping over me smoking in it, because she barely came in here in the first place.

The pool house was a miniature version of a house. It had a living room area, a kitchen, and two full-size bedrooms with a bathroom in both of them. When I was younger, and my parents started getting on my nerves about some bullshit, I would stay in here for days just to get away from them.

Inhaling the smoke in my mouth, I threw my head back and exhaled through my nose, checking my emails and messages. There wasn't shit going on but some bitches trying to get some dick tonight. It had been a couple of weeks since I had been inside some wet-wet. My first instinct was to reply back to one of them hoes, but I quickly remembered that I was trying out being faithful and shit. Damn. I was horny as fuck too. Sasha better get over her attitude and start popping some pussy for me fast. That or learn how to suck some dick.

I glanced down at my phone, and a number I didn't recognize was calling. I never answered calls from people numbers that wasn't familiar to me, so I pressed ignore and continued to smoke my blunt. The number called back again, and I answered the phone, irritated.

"Who the fuck is this!" I shouted into the phone.

"Well, hello to you too, Ron. Did you miss me as much as I missed you?" The caller laughed in the phone. I knew that high-pitched ass voice anywhere.

"Why in the fuck you playing on my motherfucking phone, Amber? I told yo' ass one time to leave me the fuck alone, but you just don't listen. I told you don't contact my mother no more, but you still did that shit. Next time I see you, you are dead, bitch. I don't care if we are out in public, I'mma kill yo' ass."

She continued to laugh. "I know you don't mean that, so I'm gon' let your outburst slide. And I don't appreciate you sending bitches to my house trying to look for me. Luckily, I don't live there anymore." I had sent some females workers to handle her, but she wasn't anywhere to be found, but I wasn't worried. I had one of my guys tracking her down as we spoke. She couldn't hide forever.

I felt like I was giving this bitch too much conversation, so I was about to end the call, but she said something that caught my attention. "That curly-head bitch that you have been dealing with is pretty. It would be a shame if something was to happen to that face of hers, if you catch my drift," Amber said, no longer laughing. Her voice held a sinister tone. "Get rid of her, or I will."

Amber threatening to do something to Sasha struck a nerve with me. I shot up from my seat like it was on fire. "Are you fucking threatening me, bitch! Yo, yo' ass play crazy, but I'm the fucking real deal. Come near my bitch and place a single hand on her; I will make it my personal mission to find you, tie you up, drive over your whole damn body five times in a row, and then shoot you in the head—all while wearing a smile on my face. Try me, bitch, if you want!" I hollered before hanging up on her dumb ass.

I pinched the brim of my nose, trying to calm down my anger as I paced the floor. She had blown my high. This bitch had the fucking audacity to not only call my phone on some stalker type shit, but then she also had the balls to threaten to do something to Sasha. I had to find this bitch like yesterday before she fucked around and followed through with what she said. There wasn't a doubt in my mind that she wasn't playing. She was too delusional.

I heard a knock then the door opened. Sasha appeared in the doorway with concern written all over her face. Seeing her pretty ass instantly calmed me down a little. Cautiously walking over to where I was standing, her eyes locked in on mine. "I heard you yelling from outside, so I came to check on you. What's the matter?"

"Nothing, just some shit I need to take care of asap." I knew if I told her the reason behind my anger, it would scare her shitless, so I held off on disclosing that information to her.

"Okay, whatever you say," she said, giving me a skeptical look. "We can leave now. I heard it was supposed to storm tonight, and I'm not trying to get caught in it," she said, brushing a loose strand of hair behind her ear.

"Give me a minute to sober up a bit," I said, raking my hand through my dreads.

She looked toward my dreads and frowned. "I think it's about time you get these things re-twisted. It's starting to look wild." She stood on her tiptoes, pulling on them. "If you want, I can do them for you."

"Word? You know how to do dreads?" I asked, somewhat surprised.

She laughed. "Yeah, and I know how to braid too. I just don't like doing it, but seeing as how I don't have anything to do, I might as well."

"Hold the fuck on. You wasn't fucking with me a few hours again, but now all of a sudden, you acting nice toward me and shit. You trying to be on some get back shit and fuck up my hair?" I accused, giving her the side eye.

"Don't get me wrong; I'm still mad at you for doing that to my friend, but it helped your case when I got to see those embarrassing baby pictures of you."

Grabbing her wrists, I couldn't help myself as I moved my body closer to hers, getting in her personal space. I peered down at her face as she looked up to mine. "Wh-what do you think yo-you are doing?" she stuttered, trying to step back. With every step backward she took, I took a step forward until her body was against the wall. Her breathing had become labored, and the lustful look in her eyes didn't go unnoticed as she waited for my next move.

I leaned my face near her ear. "I want some pussy, so I'm giving you one of two options. You either let me fuck, or give me some head," I whispered and licked around her ear. I felt her body shiver before she pushed me away from her, wearing a scowl on her face. *Oh shit, she was about to be on some bullshit,* I thought, rolling my eyes to the ceiling.

"You got me so twisted right now. You must be out of your damn mind if you think I'm going to give you some ass after that shit that you did today. And not to mention, I don't know who all you been fucking, and I ain't trying to catch nothing." She crossed her arms.

I didn't know why, but I felt offended by her assumptions. "Yo, don't fucking play me like I'm one of this nasty ass niggas that fuck raw. You know firsthand that I always wrap my shit up. And don't try to use that 'holier than thou' shit with me when it wasn't too long ago that you was fucking me, knowing that I was fucking other females," I said, airing her out.

Her eyes widened with shock. She had her eyes fixated on me for a couple of seconds. She opened her mouth to say something, but nothing came out. Instead, she shook her head, turning to walk out the door. I knew I had hurt her feelings, but the truth hurt sometimes. Still, I couldn't let her walk away from me.

I caught her before she could walk out the door, and I forcefully slammed it shut. "Oh, so your feelings are hurt now." Those were the only words I could think to say. I wasn't about to apologize for what I said, because I was speaking the truth. If she didn't like what I said, then maybe she should've thought before saying what she said.

"Please get away from me." She spoke calmly with her back still turned away from me.

"Nawl, you good where you are at now," I responded with my hands still placed on the door, preventing her from leaving. No matter how mad she was at me, I wasn't letting her leave. Matter fact, we wouldn't be leaving out this pool house until the morning.

I was pretty sure that if we left now, I would have to chase her ass down for the rest of the week to get her to talk to me again. I wouldn't admit this out loud, but I missed being around her. She had a way of easing my mind and making me forget the stress that came along with the street life. Since her back was turned to me, I took the opportunity to wrap my arms around her from the back. I felt her body tense up as she tried to jerk away from me.

"I know what I said was fucked up, but what you said to me was fucked up as well, making it seem like I'm walking around here with a nasty dick. You can't just dish shit out and not expect nothing to be said back to you. That's not how shit works," I explained. I waited for her response, but I got nothing.

I turned her around so that she was facing me. I half expected to see tears running down her face, but what I saw was much worse. I saw the same hurt in her eyes as the day that I told her we couldn't be together. "I can't believe that you said that to me," she whispered in a child-like voice, reminding me of how oversensitive she could be at times.

Staring in her face made me second guess my choice to be with her. I knew deep down that she didn't need a nigga like me in her life. I would ruin her. She needed one of those square ass niggas that had a nine to five that would appreciate her in a way I didn't think I ever could, but the selfish part me of didn't give a fuck about what I knew she needed. I just wanted her.

"Look, shit hasn't been going good between us since the day at the activity center. So I'm willing to give you what you want. If you can look me in the eyes and tell me that you don't want me to be in your life, then I'll make that happen." Just like that night in Hawaii, I was letting her make the decision to fuck with me or not.

Sasha

$\mathcal{I}$ sat at a red light, twirling around the necklace on my neck, looking out the window, and watching the cars speed past me. I had so many things on my mind, and oddly enough, painting wasn't one of them. I was on my way to Shawn's place to check up on him as well as apologize for Ron's actions yesterday. What he did was uncalled for. I knew that I would have to explain to him who Ron was and why he did what he did, even though I wasn't completely sure myself. Letting out an exasperated sigh, I had a flashback of last night and what transpired.

"Look, shit hasn't been going good between us since the outside of the activity center. So I'm willing to give you what you want. If you can look me in the eyes and tell me that you don't want me to be in your life, then I'll make that happen."

When he spoke those words, I raised my head and looked him square in the face. Though I was hurt by his word choice, I couldn't be mad at him for speaking the truth. I was the dummy who allowed him to do that shit to me. But for him to throw it in my face like that was uncalled for. He didn't even have the decency to apologize. That only proved to me that he didn't give a fuck about me.

I opened my mouth to tell him that I didn't want to be with him, but my heart stopped me. No matter how hurt I was by his words, I knew that I couldn't bring myself to say that to him. So I did what I did best. I remained silent. Secretly, I wanted him to beg me to be with him, but it didn't happen.

After about an hour of not speaking, he grabbed his keys and took me home, not uttering a word to me.

I didn't get much sleep. I spent the whole night thinking over who was the better choice for me. After much deliberation, I made my choice. I just prayed that I wouldn't regret it.

Finally, I pulled up to the house Shawn had rented for his stay here. He didn't know that I was coming over today, so I was glad to see his car parked in the driveway. I took one last deep breath before exiting the car. Knocking at the door, I waited for him to answer. When I didn't get an answer, I knocked again. The wind was blowing hard, making it difficult for me to keep warm. *Maybe he was sleep or something. I'd just come back later.* I started to walk away, but then he finally appeared at the door.

"What are you doing here?" he called out to me.

I turned around to say something, but my words were caught in my throat once I laid eyes on his appearance. He stood there with nothing but some jogging pants on. I ran over to him, placing both of my hands gently on his face. "Oh my God, look at your face!" I hysterically said. One side of his jaw was bruised, he had a band-aid on the side of his forehead, and his bottom lip was slightly swollen. Looking down at his stomach, I saw there was a huge bruise on his side. "Did you go to the doctor about this?" I asked, pointing to his side.

He removed my hands from his face. "No, I'll be good in a few days." As soon as he opened his mouth, I could smell the liquor on his breath. Now that I was standing close to him, his whole body reeked of alcohol. I found this very odd for him to be drinking in the middle of the day, but I didn't speak on it.

I followed behind him as he walked back inside. I inspected the living room, and it was dark but not dark enough that I couldn't see multiple bottles of beer scattered across his glass table and food containers everywhere. This was definitely cause for concern.

"Is everything alright with you?" I questioned in concern.

He walked into the kitchen and returned with another bottle of beer. "I'm gucci," he told me before flopping down on the couch. "So who was that dude?"

I knew that question would come sooner or later. I cleared my throat before I spoke. "Remember that day at the mall I told you about a dude I really liked, but the only problem was he was messing with other females? Well, that was him," I said softly.

Nodding his head, the only thing he said was, "Hmm."

"What's the supposed to mean?" I frowned.

"Nothing." He waved me off, downing his drink. Once he finished swallowing, he looked over to me. "Let me ask you this. Is he the reason why you haven't gave me an answer yet?"

I didn't want to tell him the truth, but I didn't want to lie to him either, so I nodded my head slowly.

"I don't know why I keep doing this shit to myself." He laughed sarcastically. I didn't know if he was talking to me or himself, so I said nothing. "Your phone is over there by the wall." He pointed. "You can leave now. I know that's the only reason you came by any damn way."

I jerked my head back. "What you mean by 'that's the only reason why I came over here'? I came to check on you."

He chuckled before taking another sip of his drink. "That's funny to me because if you were really concerned about me, then you would've stayed by my side when that nigga beat my ass and left me on the ground. Instead, you left right with his ass after he disrespected yo' ass!" he spat.

I was taken aback. I knew that he wasn't blaming me for what had transpired yesterday. "Where is all this attitude coming from? Clearly, you saw me trying to break y'all up before anything got started, and I know you saw me when I was trying to get to you, but he picked me up and carried me to his car despite me kicking and screaming. What else was I supposed to do?" I was trying to get him to see my point of view.

"You were supposed to have my fucking back!" He shot up from his seat and beelined toward me. I was in complete shock. He had never spoken to me this way, let alone shouted like this. He grabbed ahold of both my arms aggressively and slammed my back against the wall. He no longer looked like the same person. His face had a demonic-like appearance to it, and his eyes had completely gone black. At this point, I was scared shitless of what he might do to me next.

"I thought you was different, but you are just like that hoe ass bitch I almost married. Y'all don't appreciate a good man that would treat you right. Nawl, y'all want a nigga that don't give a fuck about you and treat you like shit!" he said, screaming with spit flying out his mouth.

The pain from him slamming me against the wall and squeezing the shit out my arms was too much for me. "Stop! You are hurting me!" I yelled, crying uncontrollably.

I guess seeing me cry finally got through to him. He released my arms and stepped back. No longer were his eyes black, and his face had returned back to normal. "I'm sorry, Sasha. I didn't mean to take it that far." His face showed remorse, but I didn't care. I just wanted to get up out of here. I ran to the door, grabbing my phone in the process before slamming it shut, speeding out the driveway.

I rubbed my throbbing back and arms all the way home. I couldn't process how things went so far left so fast. I wanted to make the excuse of him being drunk for the cause of his action, but I was always told a drunk mind speaks sober thoughts. Walking into my apartment, I threw the keys on the counter and made my way to the bathroom mirror to inspect the damage. Taking off my shirt, I turned my body to the left, getting a better view of my arm. Then I repeated the same movements with my right arm and back. The places where he gripped my arms were extremely red, and I could see his handprints. My back wasn't all that bad; I just couldn't make any quick movements.

I ran some hot bath water and made sure that I put Epsom salt in. Maybe it would help with the pain. I turned on some jazz music before stripping out of my clothes. Checking the temperature of the water with my toes to make sure it wasn't too hot, I got right in. As soon as my body was completely in, my muscles relaxed. Leaning my head back on the tub, I closed my eyes.

I really wanted to erase today's event out of my head. I didn't want to have any negative thoughts about Shawn. I wanted to still look at him as the same sweet person I'd always known him to be, but I knew that I wouldn't look at him the same anymore. I hated to always compare the two, but at least with Ron, I knew what I was getting into. Shawn's actions came out of left field. I wasn't even sure I wanted to talk to him, let alone be friends.

I sat in the water until it had become cold, and my skin resembled a prune. After letting out the water, I grabbed a big towel to wrap around my body and went to my bedroom to find some clothes. Once I was dressed, I lay across my bed, grabbing a notebook and a pencil from my dresser. I didn't have the energy to set up my painting area in the other room, so I opted to do something that I hadn't done in a while—sketch.

I didn't really have anything in particular that I wanted to draw. I just wanted to clear my head, and this was always the best remedy for me. An hour and three drawings later, I called it quits. I stretched my arms up in the air while I yawned. I wasn't sleepy, more so tired than anything. My phone vibrated near my feet, alerting me I had a message.

Tori: Are you down to have wine night?

Wine did sound good right now, and with the last two days I'd had, I needed some, I thought.

Me: On my way now.

I wasted no time putting on a pair of sneakers and my jacket. It took me all of twenty minutes to make it there. I was greeted at the door by Tori wearing some booty shorts that could potentially cause a yeast infection and a Victoria's Secret sports bra that looked a little bit too small for her.

"Why are you dressed like you are about to go twerk on somebody's stage?" I joked.

"Haha, I see you got jokes. You better be happy that I'm in a good mood, or I would light into yo' ass, heffa," she said, walking in front of me, digging a wedgie out of her ass.

I frowned my face in disgust. "I hope you are going to wash your hands after doing that."

She just stuck her middle finger up over her shoulders. We went into the den that was down the hall from the living room. She had two glasses filled with wine on the table, along with some cheese and crackers to go with it. Something was definitely up with her.

I gave her a suspicious look. "Okay, for real, what's going on with you?"

"Nothing, I just wanted to spend some time with my favorite cousin in the whole wide world," she said, smiling hard as hell.

I gave her a look that said 'I don't believe a word that you're saying.'

"Okay, fine. I was wondering if you wanted to take a drive with me to Dallas next weekend. I have to pick up an item, and I don't want to go by myself."

"Okay. Just don't have me caught up in no mess," I warned.

"Thank you!" she squealed, hugging me. "And here I thought

that I would have to beg you to tag along. Now that that's over with, let's start drinking, bitch," she said, downing her drink in one gulp and refilling her glass. I did the same as well.

After going through three bottles of wine, I didn't fall asleep like I normally did. Instead, I ended up on the table while Tori was trying to teach me how to twerk while music was blasting throughout the speakers in the room.

"You have to put an arch in your back and pop your hips like this while rotating yo' ass," she coached from the floor, demonstrating to me what she was talking about.

I tried mimicking her movements, but instead, I twerked my hips in an awkward motion that didn't look anything like what she showed me. It was no use anyways. I had the rhythm of a drunk white girl. I gave up after ten minutes of failing miserably.

Just as I was about to sit down, Big Sean's "So Good" came on, and I immediately got back up, shaking my non-rhythm-having ass. Tori and I rapped the song word for word while dancing in a stripper kind of way. I was ashamed to say that I actually liked this song. It wasn't my usual taste, but it was something about the lyrics and the beat that made me want to be a freak hoe.

We were having so much fun that we didn't realize that Justin, Bryan, and Ron were standing at the door until they turned off the music, making their presence known. I covered my face in embarrassment. Justin and Bryan were laughing their asses off, while Ron stood there, stoned faced, making me wonder what was going through his mind.

Once Justin noticed what Tori had on, he immediately stopped laughing and gave her an angry glare. "Aye, yo, what the fuck you think you are doing? Go put on some fucking clothes. You see my peoples here, and you got your ass and titties hanging all out and shit," he scolded her.

"Don't come in here trying to regulate shit. This is my damn house, and I can dress how I want to up in here. It's *your* fault that your friends got a sneak peek at all of this," she said in an animated voice, rubbing her hands down her body. "If you would've told me that you were bringing your friends, then maybe I would've made an attempt to at least put on a shirt." She slurred her words a little. It was clear to see that she was tipsy.

"I'mma give your drunk ass three seconds to go up them stairs to put on some motherfucking clothes before I embarrass yo' ass in front of everyone," he threatened with cold eyes. I realized that I was standing in the middle of both of them, so I politely moved to the far side. I didn't want any part of what was about to happen.

"Embarrass my ass?" she repeated his words. "Nawl. Nigga, don't make me embarrass yo' ass by telling your friends how last night, I was licking you're a—" Before she could finish her statement, he rushed toward her, covering her mouth with his hand, making her words sound muffled as he dragged her out the room.

"I'll be back. Y'all niggas betta not go any damn where either," he said, stopping at the door. "Why you always have to show yo' ass around everyone? Next time I see you bring any bottle that has liquor in it in this house, I'mma empty the shit out and buss you over the head with the empty bottle," he fussed at her.

After they left the room, Bryan, Ron, and I stood there silently before Bryan spoke what I was sure was on everyone's mind. "Please tell me she wasn't about to say she licked this nigga nasty ass?" he said to no one in particular. We all burst out in a fit of giggles. "He can't say shit else about me."

Once the laughter had died down between us, I secretly peeked at Ron. He looked extra yummy today. His dreads were freshly twisted, braided to the back. He wore a white, long-sleeved shirt with a red vest, some dark jeans, and a pair of Timberlands on his feet. He had a simple diamond necklace around his neck, and one diamond stud decorated his right ear. He checked his phone and walked out the room.

"Where you about to go? I thought we were going to play cards?" Bryan called out the door.

"I got to piss," Ron called back out. I wanted to follow behind him, but I didn't want to make it seem so obvious.

"You might as well go talk to him. You know you want to," Bryan said, taking a seat on the couch, spreading his arms out to the side of him. "Just don't fuck up these nice people's bathroom," he joked, wearing a smile on his face. I was getting the vibe that he was the jokester out of their crew.

I offered a small smile to him before heading out the door. I didn't know which particular bathroom he had gone in, so I started from the one that was located near the basement. Pressing my ear against the door, I listened for any type of sounds or movements. When I didn't hear anything, I opened the door to discover it was empty. I repeated the same process with the other two doors until I found the one that he was in.

Without knocking, I opened the door, and my mouth starting salivating as I walked in and got a glimpse of his dick before he stuffed it back in his pants. Just the sight of that thing had my juices flowing and had me ready to pounce on him. I had to cross my legs just to control my urge. The lust must've shown on my face, because he looked at me and gave me that infamous sexy smirk before going over to the sink and washing his hands, never once speaking a word to me.

I made my way toward him, not stopping until I had gotten close enough to stand on my tiptoes and wrap my hands around his neck. He raised an eyebrow, and I was pretty sure he was wondering what I was about to do, but he didn't stop me. Crushing my lips against his, I hungrily kissed him. He didn't waste any time returning the gesture.

I slid my tongue in his mouth, which he gladly sucked on. I didn't realize how much I missed the feeling of his lips against mine until now. He snaked his large hands around my ass, pushing me close to his body, not leaving any space between us before giving both cheeks a squeeze, followed by a hard smack, turning me on even more. I grinded my pelvic area against his dick, causing it to brick up. Without notice, he lifted my body up in the air and set me on the counter without breaking our kiss. I took the opportunity to push his pants down enough to reach in his boxers and free his dick.

"Don't pull that motherfucker out if you don't plan to do anything with it," he stated seriously.

Instead of responding, I bit my bottom lip, stroking the length of his dick with my hands, resuming our kiss.

I didn't know if it was the alcohol I had consumed or the fact that I needed to feel him that made me this bold, but I didn't give a damn. He soon abandoned my lips, licking his way down to my neck before latching onto it. I let out a soft moan in response to his action. He had long ago found that my neck was one of my hot spots. Getting tired of foreplay, he started removing my leggings and panties from underneath my butt. He finally got them off and threw them on the floor. Opening the drawer to the right of us, he pulled out a box of condoms and removed one.

"Really?" I asked with a look of disbelief. It seemed like this man had a box of condoms stashed everywhere.

"If you stay ready, you'll never have to get ready." He smiled, placing it on his member.

Closing my eyes, I braced myself as I felt the base of his dick at my entrance. It had been awhile since he had been inside of me, so I knew I was about to experience some pain.

"Open your eyes," he commanded. I did as he told me, looking into his beautiful hazel eyes.

He did a slow grind so it could be easier to enter me. He did this for a couple of seconds before he finally slid in. My mouth had opened, but no sounds came out as he started to long stroke me. He wasn't showing my body any mercy with the way he was pounding in and out of me. Placing my hands on his stomach, I tried pushing him back, but he just slapped my hands away.

"Nawl, ma. You gon' take this dick," he growled through his strokes. It wasn't long before I felt an orgasm building up inside me.

Three strokes later, I came hard on his dick. He wasted no time lifting me up and turning me around so he could enter me from the back.

I let out a loud moan. "I can feel it in my stomach." I squirmed, trying to get away. He just grabbed both of my arms and held them behind my back. I moaned uncontrollably as he proceeded to assault my vagina. He was stroking me so good that I had tears threatening to fall down. I raised my head up as I caught him staring at our reflection through the mirror.

His face held no expression, but his eyes told a different story. There was so much passion behind them. I saw something else behind them as well. I just couldn't quite make out what exactly it meant.

He plunged deep inside of me, bringing me back to reality. It felt like he had buried himself balls deep inside of me. I cried out as he attacked my spot over and over again. My vagina locked down on his dick, and my legs began to feel weak. Another orgasm surfaced, taking over my whole body. Ron pumped viciously behind me until he finally came.

"Damn," he whispered so low that I barely heard him. We stayed in this postilion until our breathing became normal. I winced at the pain that I felt when slid himself out of me.

My legs gave out, and I fell to the floor. I didn't have enough energy to get up, so I just lay there with my eyes closed and my legs open. After he flushed the condom down the toilet, I felt him standing over me.

"Get yo' ass up off this floor and put back on your clothes."

"I can't," I whined. "I'm too tired to do anything."

I heard him chuckling. Soon after, I heard water running and felt a warm towel in between my legs. My eyes shot open as I looked down and watched him clean me off. This was definitely a first. I wanted to ask why he was doing this, but I didn't want to risk the chance of him stopping. The warm towel was easing the pain I felt on my other set of lips.

Once he was done, he threw the towel in the tub and helped me up. My legs were still a little wobbly, but at least I could stand up now. I was sure my panties were soaking wet, so I didn't even bother to put them back on.

As I was putting on my leggings, I noticed that he was leaning against the door with his arms folded, staring at me. "Why are you staring at me like that?" I nervously asked.

"Just noticed that your ass gotten a little bigger. When I was hitting it from the back, I saw that it started to jiggle."

I grinned at him. "My little booty finally got a little bounce to it, huh?" I joked, shaking it a bit, causing him to let out a laugh.

"Don't let what I said go to your head. Yeah, it was jiggling a little, but you got a long way to go if you want to cause some waves."

"Whatever." I giggled. When I was done dressing and washing my hands, he opened the door to walk out, but I stopped him. Placing my hands gently on top of his, I looked into his eyes. "I think I need to explain a few things before we leave out of here. First, I want to start off by saying that I didn't mean it when I said I hated you. I don't have it in me to hate anyone, especially you. I was just speaking out of anger. I was still in my feelings about how you treated me and what you did to

Shawn. And just for the record, I never slept with him."

He scowled at the mention of his name, but I continued with my speech.

"When you ask me to give you an answer regarding if I wanted you out of my life or not, my first thought was to say yes for all the stuff you did to me, but I couldn't, and I was confused as to why I couldn't say it. That's why I didn't say anything. Last night, I couldn't sleep, thinking over what I wanted. I can name a million reasons why I shouldn't be with you, but I also can name a million reason why I should, so I wondered if maybe the offer still stands…" I hesitated, feeling vulnerable. I held my breath, awaiting his answer.

Ron stared at me, expressionless, as if he weren't fazed by what I said. We stood there for what seemed like hours. I was starting to feel stupid for confessing to him and potentially getting played again. I fought the urge to cry. I was done crying over men. For the last couple of months, that's what I'd been doing, and I refused to let it happen again. Breaking eye contact, I turned my head away, but he touched my chin, turning me to face him.

"Aight, it's official. You locked a nigga down." He smiled but then grew serious. "Don't make me catch a body out here over you, Sasha." He pulled me into his strong arms, hugging me. I hugged him back, burying my face in his chest. He kissed me on the forehead.

He pulled away. "Let's get the fuck out of here before those nosy ass people come looking for us." I nodded my head in agreement, allowing him to pull me out by my hand.

Everything about this moment felt so right. I wasn't choosing

Ron based off what happened with Shawn today. I was choosing Ron because he was where my heart was at. I didn't fully understand the reason behind it, and maybe I didn't need to. I mean, after all, wasn't that what love was all about?

We walked back to the den, trying not to give off any indication of what just happened in the bathroom. Justin and Bryan were seated at the table in the corner, shuffling cards, and a more clothed Tori was on the couch, pouting, watching TV. Once we walked in the room, their attention turned toward us, and Bryan immediately went in.

"Don't come in here looking all innocent and shit. We heard your freaky ass in the bathroom moaning and shit." My face grew hot. *Oh my gosh, they heard us.* He looked toward Ron. "Nigga, what were you doing to that girl in there? I was tempted to call 9-1-1 with the way you had her screaming."

I turned around, hiding my face in his shirt in embarrassment. "What you think I was doing in that bitch? I was making her feel like a real nigga supposed to make his bitch feel. Now if are you done worrying about what the fuck I do with my dick, let's play some cards." That was his response.

I removed my head from his chest and gave him a death stare, but he just winked at me before going over to the table to play cards. I took a seat next to Tori, laying my head on her shoulder.

"Wait, did this nigga just say 'his bitch'?" Bryan asked, looking around the room at everyone. "Oh, hell nawl! Hell must be frozen over if this nigga in a relationship. I should've been asking *you* what you did to *him* while y'all was in there," he said to me.

I laughed, shaking my head. I didn't want to have any part in this conversation.

"Nigga, shut the fuck up and throw out a damn card," Justin said. "While you worried about other people getting pussy, you need to find some that won't have you taking a trip to the clinic."

Bryan leaned his head back a little. "I was waiting for you to say something so I could lay into that ass. Pause. You shut the hell up with yo' *like getting the booty ate* ass. But seriously, I want to know what part of the game that is. I mean, do you get on all fours, or do you have your legs in the air like a bitch?"

I bit the inside of my mouth, fighting hard to keep from laughing. I prayed nobody else laughed out loud, because I would definitely lose the battle. I was thankful no one did, but I could tell from their faces that they were struggling to not laugh as well.

"You can't say a damn thing to me when we had to pick yo' ass up in the middle of nowhere while you stood in the road butt naked with leaves covering yo' black ass. Knowing your ass, you probably tried to get freaky with one of those animals out there, and they ended up fucking you up."

I was the first one to laugh, followed by everyone else. I laughed so hard that my stomach started to cramp, and I couldn't breathe. Even Ron was holding his stomach, laughing.

They continued to go back and forth, talking about each other, until I almost passed out from laughing at them. Tori and I walked out the room, done with their shenanigans.

"Damn, that nigga must've really put it on you, got you limping and shit." Tori laughed behind me.

"Girl, bye," I said, trying to play it off. Once we entered the kitchen, she went straight to the fridge to grab two bottles of water, tossing me one. I took a seat on the bar stool, careful not to hurt myself.

"So y'all made things official, huh?" She smiled, leaning over the counter. I nodded my head, gulping down my water. "I knew that you would choose Ron," she stated matter-of-factly.

"Why did you think that?"

"Let me see how I can explain this." She looked up with her index finger rubbing her chin. "Okay, I got it. Though they are both sexy as fuck, Ron has something that Shawn lacks, which is seasoning."

"Seasoning? I'm not following you." I was genuinely confused.

"Let's say they are both two separate boxes of chicken. Ron is like fried chicken that was cooked right and had the perfect amount of seasoning. Sure, it's bad for you, but it tastes good. On the other hand, Shawn is like baked chicken with no seasoning at all. It's the healthier choice, but it's not as appealing. In other words, he is boring and don't have any excitement to him."

"No, it doesn't have anything to do with him being boring. It's just timing. If Shawn would've came in my life before Ron, I would've…" My voice trailed off, and I unconsciously rubbed my arms where he had left a bruise. Would I have chosen Shawn if Ron wasn't in the picture?

"You would've what?"

I shook my head. "Nothing, but what about you and the whole eating ass thing?" I questioned, trying the subject.

She waved me off. "Girl, that was my first time doing that to his ass. I had just got done watching a porno, and I wanted to try it on him. I started sucking his dick and slowly made my way to his ass, literally." She laughed at her own joke, but I didn't find it funny. "I only got five licks in before that nigga jumped off the bed and cursed me out to everything he could think of. He was dead ass mad. He even made my ass sleep in another room."

I turned my nose up, scooting my bottle far away from her. "You keep your bottle over there, and you are no longer allowed to drink out any of my cups either." I pointed to the end of the counter.

She stuck up her middle finger at me, rolling her eyes. "Whatever. I just hope you clean my bathroom before you leave. I'm the only one that can leave my pussy juice around this house."

"I never realized how disgusting you were."

"Sorry to break it to you, but I am a nasty bitch and proud of it. If you stick around, you might learn a thing or two." She winked. "Now, on to important business. Thanksgiving is next month, and all I want to know is, which one of us will be driving to Georgia?

"What you mean, which one of us? I drove to and back from there last year. It's your turn now."

"Damn, you know I'm not a morning person. Okay, let's make a deal. You drive there, and I'll drive back."

"Only if you ask Justin if we can take his Mercedes truck." I always wanted to drive that car, but he made it perfectly clear that he was the only person that could drive it. Any other car, he didn't care about.

"You know how much begging, pleading, fucking, and sucking

I'mma have to do to get him agree to that?"

I shrugged my shoulders. That was the only way that I would do it, so if she didn't want to drive, then she better start begging like Keith Sweat.

"Deal," she finally agreed. We sat around for close to two hours, talking and feeding our faces.

Finally, the men came out of the den with their eyes low, smelling like the strongest weed. Ron nodded his head to the side, motioning for me to come to him.

"Come take a ride with me," he said once I made it over to him.

"To where?"

"What I tell you about asking so many damn questions? I'm your nigga, right?" He paused to allow me to answer. I nodded my head. "So trust me. Now come on," he stated firmly.

I followed behind him out the door. He unlocked the car door, and we both got in. It didn't take long before we pulled in front of a big house that had four cars parked out front. *This better not be another relative's house he took me to,* I thought.

I almost had a heart attack when he took me to his parents' home. Meeting parents always caused me anxiety, not that I met a whole bunch of them, but I met enough to realize that I didn't like it. Though a lot of people would argue and say that the parents' opinions didn't matter, it did. They had a way of making or breaking a relationship. I knew from personal experience.

"You can stop looking like that. This is my crib. You are the only female besides my mama that know where I live, so you should feel honored. Now get yo' ass out," he commanded.

I got out and caught up to him. We entered the house together. He gave a quick tour around the place. He had a huge kitchen that could fit at least thirty to forty people in it. The living room was even bigger. There were four bedrooms with a unique design to each one and bathrooms that gave a hotel suite a run for their money. Also, he had a built-in movie theater. Whoever decorated his house did a damn good job. Don't get me wrong; a person could tell that it was a man's home, but it had a feminine touch to it as well.

"Why did you buy a house this big when it's only you that lives here?" I couldn't help but ask, cuddling up next to him while he lay in the bed with one of his hands behind his head. He used the other hand to flip through channels.

"I've always lived in a big house. I wasn't about to downgrade just because I was living by myself," he answered nonchalantly.

He lifted his shirt a little to scratch his stomach, revealing the scar he had received due to the accident. I traced up and down the scar gently, careful not to apply any pressure. "Does it still hurt?"

He broke his attention away from the show he was watching to look at his scar. "Not really, but then again, it hasn't fully healed either. The doctor said I should be good by next month."

"I was scared when I heard about the accident," I revealed. I thought that you..." My voice trailed off as I went back to that moment when I got the call from Tori. I shook off the negative thoughts that had formed in my head.

"Kill that sad shit," he demanded. "You are here laying in bed with me. That's all you need to focus on, with yo' emotional ass. I'mma have to toughen you up. You can't be my bitch and be a crybaby. That shit just doesn't match."

I frowned at his choice of words. "I need you not refer to me as *your bitch*." I let it slide at Tori's house and when he fought Shawn, but I wasn't about to do it again. "Say your woman or lady—something in that nature. Anything but bitch. It's a derogatory term."

He wasn't even listening to me, because he was too busy laughing at whatever he was watching. I hit him hard enough to get his attention.

"Chill with that hitting shit. I heard yo' whiny ass complaining about being called my bitch. If it will make you happy and shut you the fuck up so I can enjoy this show, then I won't call you that anymore. Happy now?"

"Not until you give me a kiss," I said, puckering my lips, purposely trying to annoy him.

"Maybe I need to reconsider this relationship shit. You are already working on my damn nerves," he complained, but he still gave me a kiss.

I was smiling on the inside at my small victory. I knew that it would take some time for me to get him to tap into his emotional side that I knew that was buried deep, deep down in his body, but I was up for the challenge.

****

Tapping my finger against the wooden table, I checked my phone for the time. Shawn had been blowing my phone up for the past three weeks straight to get me to talk to him. At first, I was against it, but after some thought, I felt like that was the least that I could do, but I made it completely clear that we had to meet in a public area. I wasn't taking any chances of him putting his hands on me again. The two bruises he left on both of my arms had gone away, but not before Ron got a glimpse of one while I was changing clothes.

When he asked me what happened, I thought of a quick lie and told him that I hit it against the door frame while taking out the trash. I didn't think he fully believed me, but he let it go. I knew it may seem as if I was covering for Shawn, which maybe I was. But knowing the person that he was, I genuinely felt like he didn't mean it, but I wasn't going to let him off the hook that easily either.

I finally saw him strolling through the door with his eyes searching for me. I raised my hand, and he spotted me and began to walk over. Once he had taken a seat in front of me, I took in his appearance. He wasn't his normal smiling, put-together self. He looked as if he were broken. He wore a grim look on his face with dark circles under his eyes like he hadn't slept for days, and his eyes were filled with sadness.

An awkward silence lingered between us, neither one of us knowing what to say. After sitting there for five minutes, just looking around, Shawn finally spoke. He cleared his throat. "First, I just want to apologize for the other week. I had no right to do what I did to you, and I've been fucked up over it since then." I could see the regret on his face.

"I came by your house to apologize for what went down, but you just blew up on me, and then you compared me to your ex. Is that how you really feel about me?"

He shifted uncomfortably in his seat before making eye contact with me. "Umm, not exactly," he stumbled. "I did mean it when I said that women always pass over good men and run straight to the ones that aren't good for them. I am a prime example of that. Throughout my whole life, I thought that girls were after men with good looks, so when I'd gotten through my awkward-looking stage, I thought I was going to have women flocking over me. It did happen, but they didn't stay around for long even though I treated them how a man's supposed to treat a woman. After that, it didn't take me long to realize that women wanted men that didn't give a shit about them. Even with my ex, I treated her like a queen, but she still cheated on me."

"But that still doesn't explain why you said that to *me*," I emphasized, pointing to my chest. "You, of all people, should know that I'm not like that."

"I know, but you do have to admit that the guy that showed up that day was hella disrespectful and an asshole." I giggled a little. I definitely couldn't argue with that. "After y'all left, I went home and started thinking about all the females that did me wrong, and that lead me to drinking the whole night. I guess I just took my anger out on you because I felt like you had thrown me away like the rest of those women did, but I swear I didn't mean to put my hands on you. Even though I was in my feelings, that still doesn't excuse my actions. I was raised better than to hit a woman."

"Yes, you were. You better be lucky I didn't tell your mother what you did to me." When I saw his eyes widen, I burst out laughing. "Don't worry, I'm not, but if you let it happen again, I will right after I cut you."

"So are we good now?" he asked.

I thought about it for a minute. I understood the fact that his anger was coming from a place of being hurt, and I could tell he was remorseful, so how could I not forgive him? We were all humans and made mistakes "We're good," I replied before kicking his leg as hard as I could from under the table.

"Ouch!" He frowned, rubbing his leg under the table.

"Now we are really good." I smiled, and just like that, everything was back to normal between us. We talked for close to an hour before I got a text from Ron.

Ron: *Meet me at the crib in 30 mins.*

Me: *Why?*

Ron: *I told you about doing that shit. Do as I say and meet me there.*

Exiting out my messages, I looked over to Shawn and told him I had to leave. I moved the chair back and stood up from my seat, gathering my things. I turned to walk away when he grabbed my arm, stopping me in my tracks.

"Did I ever have a chance with you?" he nervously questioned, looking me in the eyes.

"If you would've told me how you felt about me years ago, then yes, I think things would've worked out between us. But you waited too long, and I fell in love with someone else," I replied truthfully.

Nodding his head, he got up from his seat as well. "I understand.

Maybe I should've voiced my feelings in high school instead of doubting myself and being a pussy." He laughed, but the hurt was evident in his voice.

"I'm pretty sure that you will find a female that goes just as hard as you will for her. You are a great person, Shawn. Don't let anyone else tell you differently. Who knows? If things don't work out in my relationship, I might be first in line, beating down your door, trying to get with you," I said, trying to lighten up the mood and make him feel better.

"I'm holding you to that," he said, following me out the door. Like always, he walked me over to my car and held the door for me to get in and closed it behind me. "Drive safe," he called out from outside the window.

I waved before pulling off. I was relieved that we had gotten everything resolved, and things were good between us, and I had my friend back once again. Maybe in a different life, we would've been perfect for one another, but in this one, my heart belonged to Ron. I prayed that he found the happiness that he longed for because he truly deserved it.

Making it to Ron's house, I used the key he had given me to let myself in because he claimed that he was tired of me interrupting him while he was out handling business to come let me in, but I thought otherwise. I had been sleeping over here for the past couple of nights because it was closer to my job, so I didn't have to wake up as early as I normally did. If I was being honest with myself, I loved waking up to Ron's body close to mine.

Most days, he would just be getting into bed minutes before I had to wake up and get ready, but I never disturbed him as he slept. I had made the mistake of doing that one time before, and this nigga nearly tore my head off. From that moment on, I swore never to do that again. I didn't bother to call his name and ask what room he was in. I already had a pretty good idea of where I could find him.

I climbed the stairs headed toward the master bedroom. I walked in and heard the shower on. Looking around the room, I saw a couple of bags on the floor and a gorgeous, long, red and white dress laying neatly on the bed. I walked over to get a better look, and it was even more beautiful up close. I ran my hands up and down the soft, silk material, wondering what was going on.

I tried waiting patiently until Ron got out the shower to start my line of questioning, but I wanted to know now. Bursting in the bathroom, I pulled open the glass door to the huge shower and almost forgot why I had come in there in the first place. The site before me was mesmerizing. He had his back turned toward me, giving me a view of his manly buns. The combination of water and soap bubbles falling down his sexy body was enough to make me wish I was one of them just for a moment.

"You can either get in with me so I can fuck you or close the shower door because you are letting that cold air in." He finally turned around to look at me. It didn't take me long to make up my mind when I caught sight of his penis standing at full attention. I didn't waste any time stripping out of my clothes and putting my curls in a loose bun before getting in.

As soon as I stepped in, he attacked my lips while caressing my body. He grabbed a handful of my ass and squeezed it before sliding a finger into my vagina from the back. I let out a soft moan, enjoying the feeling of his finger sliding in and out while he sucked on my neck and licked on my ears. He pressed a button on the side, and the water stopped running.

Grabbing both of my legs, he picked me up and laid my body on the shower floor. He kissed my lips again before lowering his head to leave a trail of soft kisses from my neck, to my breasts, and to my stomach, stopping just above my pussy. I thrust my pelvic area in an upward motion, trying to give him a hint to continue, but I felt nothing. I pushed my body up with my elbow to see what the what the holdup was.

As soon as we made eye contact, his mouth latched onto my clit, and my eyes nearly rolled to the back of my head. He moved his tongue as if he were turning a light switch on and off as he licked and sucked my most intimate area. Not being able to withstand the pleasure I was receiving, I tried scooting my body backward, but he had a death grip on my thighs.

I screamed out in pleasure when I felt a huge orgasm rip through my body. Ron wasted no time picking my body up, placing me against the door, and entering me, causing me to gasp. Though Ron and I had been going at it like rabbits lately, I was still having a hard time fully getting adjusted to his size. I leaned my head forward, biting his shoulder as he continued to stroke me long and hard, showing my body no mercy. My vaginal muscles tightened around his dick as another orgasm approached.

"Hold that shit!" he demanded in my ear. I didn't know how to hold off on having an orgasm, but I would try. Instead of focusing on the pleasure he was giving me, I looked at the glass door, trying to distract myself from cumming, but it was no use. His kept hitting my spot back to back, and I could no longer hold it.

"Ohhhhh, I'm cumming!" I screamed to the top of my lungs, letting my juices cover his dick. I felt his dick hardening inside of me, and he pulled out, releasing himself on the shower floor. Our bodies slid down while we tried to catch our breath.

He turned the water back on, and we washed each other's bodies while we exchanged kisses. "We have somewhere to be in the next two hours, so I'mma need you to finish washing up and get dressed. I want you to wear the dress you saw laying on the bed. Inside of the bags on the floor are some heels to wear. Since I don't know shit about heels, I asked the lady that worked at the place what would she recommend, and she chose those three pairs. So whichever one of those bitches you like, wear it," he told me, getting out the shower.

I nodded my head. *What did he have up his sleeve?* I thought to myself as I finished up.

Once I had slathered my body with lotion and brushed my teeth, I walked in to see Ron wearing a tuxedo, looking good enough to eat. After I was done dressing and styling my hair, I was ready to go but not before I took a picture of both of us together. I wasn't going to post it on social media or anything. I was very private when it came to my personal life, and posting pictures of my relationship was out of the question.

When he made it outside, I was shocked to see a black limo waiting for us. The chauffeur opened the door for us to get in, and we were off. I stared a hole in Ron's head, waiting for him to tell me where we were going, but he never looked my way. He just texted on his phone the whole time. I fought the urge to question him, knowing that he wasn't going to tell me anything, so I just took a deep breath and remained quiet until we got to where we were going.

An hour later, we were pulling up outside of a museum where a large crowd had gathered, mingling amongst themselves. There were lights and cameras flashing everywhere, and there was even a red carpet. Everyone was dressed so glamorous from head to toe. If I could describe the scene before my eyes, I would compare it to something out of a big Hollywood movie premiere. I definitely needed answers now.

"What's going on, and why are we here?" I asked with my arms folded and a raised eyebrow.

He smiled before intertwining our hands. "You'll find out soon enough," he said just as the door popped open, and he stepped out, pulling me along with him.

Once the crowd saw us, they grew silent. All eyes were on us, and I couldn't help but feel out of place. I held Ron's hand a little tighter to keep myself from jumping back into the limo. He peered down at me, giving me a reassuring smile before we walked through the double glass doors. My heart nearly dropped when I saw all of my paintings hanging up on the walls of the museum. Just as I was about to speak, I saw a man walk from the back.

I nearly fainted when I saw Daniel Glazer, one of the biggest art dealers around the world and my idol. Everything this man touched turned to gold. Not only did he own over three hundred art museums worldwide, but he was also an artist as well.

"It's nice to finally put a face with the talented woman who put together some of the most amazing pieces that I have seen over the past couple of years," he complimented me with a smile, waiting for me to shake his hands. I was so star struck that it took Ron nudging me to realize Daniel's hand was out. I nervously shook it, still not believing that this wasn't a dream.

"It's nice to meet you. I am one of your biggest fans," I heard myself say, sounding like a teenager that had just met her celebrity crush.

"I think I should be the one telling you that. When Kevin told me that his son wanted to meet with me about a talented artist he knew, I wasn't expecting much. In my line of work, a lot of people think they have the gift to draw, but art is more than drawing; it's a desire to create things based off your feelings and emotions. Most people don't understand that, but you, my dear, get it. When I look at your piece, it shakes something inside of me. I haven't felt that feeling in a long time, and if you are interested, I would love to partner with you. I have a strong feeling that we could do great things together."

I stood there, speechless. No way possible could *the* Daniel Glazer be here, standing right in front of me, asking if we could work together. I had prayed so many nights for this moment to happen, and it had finally come true.

I covered my mouth as tears rolled down my face. Ron grabbed me into a hug, and I cried in his chest. It took only a few seconds for me to regain my composure and finally give him an answer.

"Yes, I would love to work with you." I smiled.

"Splendid. I already got your information, and I will send over the contract so you can look over it sometime next week." He clapped his hand together excitedly. "Now that we've got that over with, it's time for people to see how amazing your work is. Guard, let them through!" he called out. The guard nodded his head before opening the door to allow the people standing outside access.

Moments later, the place was flooded with people. I stood by Daniel nervously as he introduced me as the person responsible for the *beautiful paintings that would take a person's breath away with one look.* The crowd started clapping and cheering for me. After the introductions, I moved around the room, observing people's reactions as well as their thoughts on it. So far, I was hearing a bunch of positive feedback that had me over the moon.

My eyes danced around the room for Ron. I hadn't seen him since he told me he had to use the restroom, and that was a while ago. I finally spotted him in the corner as he talked to Justin, Bryan, and Tori. I didn't even know that they were here.

"How long have you guys been here?" I asked excitedly, hugging Tori, Justin, and then Bryan. Ron walked behind me, wrapping his arms around my stomach before kissing my neck.

"We just got here about thirty minutes ago. It would've been sooner if Tori wasn't taking her damn time getting ready like it was her event," Justin complained.

She rolled her eyes. "You can't rush perfection. Anyways, I'm so happy for you!" she gushed. "You finally got what you always dreamed about. Just don't forget about us little people when you make it big," she joked.

"How could I ever forget my favorite cousin?" I smiled at her.

"Yeah, this shit does look dope," Justin commented, and they all nodded their heads.

"I told y'all niggas that my baby got talent. Now everybody about to find that shit out," Ron boasted with pride.

"Yeah, yeah, yeah, she got skills, but where is the food? And I hope they ain't serving none of those ant-size ham sandwich. Fucking around with me, I'mma mess around and eat up all them bitches." Bryan sounded a little bit too loud.

"We can't take yo' ass nowhere without you embarrassing us." Justin groaned.

"Embarrassing? Nigga, have you looked in the mirror at that tight ass suit you got on? Now that's embarrassing," he shot back, walking over to the table the food was on.

Two hours later, the crowd had died down, and I was ready to go. It was after one in the morning, and I was in serious need of sleep. I said my goodbyes to Daniel and the guests before heading out to the limo.

"Did you have a good time?" he asked me as soon as we got in the limo.

"Yes, I did, and I owe it all to you." I kissed his lips. "How do you even know Daniel, and how did you manage to pull all of this off?" It still felt surreal that all this was happening to me.

"Daniel and my dad are friends, so I told my dad that I wanted to meet with him about you. I stole a few of your paintings from your wall to show him, and I let your work speak for itself. He was sold from that point on and wanted to meet you that day. But I had a better idea." He grabbed my hand, placing a kiss on top before continuing on with the story. "I called in a few favors to book the museum we were in, and Daniel rounded up some of his people, and there you have it," he said like it wasn't a big deal.

"Thank you so much for what you did for me tonight. You didn't have to go out of your way to set all this up, but you did. I know that you aren't the type to voice your feelings, but this speaks volumes to me. I don't know how I will ever repay you, but I will find a way to if it's the last thing I do." The water works started again. "I love you." It was the first time that I had said those words to him.

He looked stunned by my confession then pulled me into his body. I wasn't expecting him to say it back, because he hated talking about the way he felt when it came to his emotions. Instead, he let his actions speak, and from that alone, I knew the feeling was mutual.

Ron

$\mathcal{I}$ stood in the doorway, watching Sasha lie on my bed with a notepad in her hands, concentrating on whatever she was doing. I had to take a moment to admire her. Even though she was dressed down in a pair of shorts, one of my T-shirts, and her curly hair all over her head, she still looked beautiful to me. It wasn't just her looks that made her beautiful. It was her personality as well.

She had a caring nature about her that balanced out my *no fucks given* attitude, and she was a cool ass chick to be around. She wasn't about the drama, and she barely complained about stupid shit like I thought she would. We hadn't had a chance to spend much time together since I had finally decided to get out the game.

I had been working non-stop, trying to tie up some loose ends, but I wasn't stressing about the shit. I knew it was the only way for me to get out. Sasha had been busy like crazy since she signed with Daniel. For the past month, she had been meeting other artists, traveling, and painting her ass off. Her work ethic went harder than a lot of these niggas out here. I was proud to say I had an ambitions bitch on my hands.

Walking in the room, I threw a small box at her, hitting the side of her legs. She grabbed the box, holding it in her hands with a frown on her face. "Why did you throw a box of condoms at me?" she asked confusedly.

"That is my last box of condoms. After we finish up this box, I'm raw dogging, so I would advise you to get on the shot or pill that y'all females get on to prevent y'all from getting pregnant."

She laughed, but I was serious as a heart attack. It didn't feel right anymore, hitting her pussy with a condom on after I slid up in her pussy raw a couple of weeks back. I saw why niggas went crazy over that shit. Don't get the shit twisted; Sasha would be the only woman that I slid up in without wearing shit for two reasons. One, I was the only nigga that had been inside of her; two, I trusted her, and that's saying something within itself because I didn't trust any bitch besides my mama.

She stopped laughing once she saw that I was serious. "Sorry to break it to you, but condoms will be our only method of birth control. I'm not about to put that stuff in my body and have some long-term effects. I've watched way too many documentaries on that stuff. So we either continue to use protection, or your pull-out game better be hella strong," she sassed, rolling her neck like Tori.

I hoped Tori's funky ass attitude wasn't rubbing off on her, because I'd be damn if I put up with half the shit that Justin went through with that bitch.

"Check that neck rolling shit. It ain't that serious for you to be doing that extra stuff." I glared at her. "Now since yo' ass want to be stubborn, I guess we both are going to find out how strong or weak my pull-out game is. If you, by chance, get pregnant, I'm letting you know

now that you ain't having no fucking abortion. So be prepared to have a crying ass baby calling you mama."

She rolled her eyes. "Yes, daddy," she said sarcastically before going back to what she was doing.

I grabbed both of her legs, sliding her body toward the edge of the bed. I climbed on top of the bed and placed myself between her legs and started nibbling on her neck. "I love when you call me that shit," I said, grinding against her, making her open her legs wider, causing my dick to brick up. It had been two days since I'd been inside of her, and my dick was dying to go into his favorite place.

"No, I have to finish this sketch." She moaned against my ears.

"You can finish that shit later," I said, yanking her notepad out of her hand and tossing it on the floor. Just as I felt her giving in, her phone starting ringing. "Let that bitch ring," I told her, pushing down her shorts.

"It's my mother." She removed my hands from her and tried to sit up, but I pushed her right back down. I pressed accept on her phone and placed it on speaker.

"Hey, Mom. What's up?" she answered, trying to sound normal, but I had something for that ass. I slid a finger inside of her pussy and began moving it in and out of her. She covered her mouth to muffle her moans.

"I was calling to see when I should expect the arrival of you and Tori for thanksgiving," her mother said.

My ears perked up. This was my first time hearing about her going home for Thanksgiving. Granted, we hadn't had much time to talk about shit, but still…

She tried closing her legs to get me to stop. I yanked them bitches right back open, but I did slow down my pace a little so she could give a response.

"We are leaving next Tuesday morning, so we should be there that night."

"Are you in the middle of working out? You sound out of breath."

"No, ummm, I, ummmm, I'm just stretching." Sasha stumbled over her words.

"What type of stretching you doing that got you breathing like that?" she questioned.

She leaned her upper body off the bed, pleading with her eyes for me to stop. I removed my finger from her pussy. "It was yoga, but I'm done now."

That's what you think, I thought before pulling down my boxers and ramming my dick inside of her. She let out a loud scream before I covered her mouth with my hands, trying to silence her moans while stroking her.

"What the hell was that!" her mother shouted into the phone. Since her ass couldn't respond. I did it for her.

"Hey, Mrs. Braley. This is Ron, Sasha's boyfriend. How are you doing?" I greeted.

"Oh, hey, Ron. It's good to finally talk to you. For a minute there, I thought you were a part of Sasha's imagination," she joked.

Sasha's pussy was gripping my dick so good I had to bite down on the bottom of my lip, trying to control myself. "I'm very much real."

"I just had a thought. You should come down with Sasha so we can officially meet, and I can thank the man that's helping my baby achieve her dream."

That wasn't such a bad idea. I mean, it wasn't like my family did shit for Thanksgiving but sit around all down day, doing nothing, so why not? I looked down at Sasha's face to see how she felt about her mother inviting me to meet her family, but I didn't think she was even listening. She was too busy concentrating on catching her nut.

"I would love to come," I responded.

"That's good to hear," she said cheerfully. "Can you put Sasha back on the phone so I can tell her bye?" she asked.

"She can hear you. The phone is on speaker."

"Oh, bye, Sasha. I'll talk to you later. I know y'all young people are trying to spend some time together, and I don't want to interrupt. I love you."

I stopped stroking and removed my hands from her mouth. "Love you too," she said, somewhat in her normal tone. Pushing the end button on her phone, I threw it to the side and went straight to work on her ass.

Thirty minutes later, I pulled out, releasing my seeds on her stomach. I could tell by her face that she was tired after the shit that we just did. She lay there naked with her body spread across the bed, breathing hard as fuck. I went to the bathroom to get a towel to wipe my sperm off her. Once I was done, I lay next to her, placing her head on my chest.

"You good?" I questioned after not hearing her say anything for a while.

She slowly nodded her head against my chest, still not mumbling a word. We stayed like this, not saying a word, just enjoying each other's presence.

She ran her hands up and down my stomach. "Why don't you have any tattoos?"

"Tattoos really ain't my shit. I'm not saying that I'm against it or no shit like that, but I'm not about to let someone put anything on my body that doesn't hold value to it. If I decide to get one in the future, I want it to be some shit that I would never regret looking at," I said, leaving out the fact that I told myself the only thing that would ever go on my body was my wife and kids' names. Before Sasha, I didn't see myself ever having either one, but being with her had me thinking differently about the shit. I found myself thinking more about having a future with her lately.

"That's crazy. I told myself the exact same thing," she said, playing with what little stomach hair I did have. "You know what else is crazy?"

Running my hair through her soft ass hair, I asked, "What?"

"Us being like this. I mean, could you have imagined almost a year ago that we could be together? No offense, I thought you were one of the rudest, most arrogant, and most shallow men that walked the face of the earth, but now I see that it's more to you than that. Of course, you still possess those characteristic traits, but not as much as before."

I wanted to say some mushy ass shit back to her, but I wasn't at that point to express my feelings yet. Like that night she told me she loved me, I was taken aback by her confession; not because of what she said, but the fact that when she spoke those words, something happened inside of me. Like a nigga legit had butterflies and shit in my stomach, and that scared the fuck out of me. It was at that moment I knew that she held the power to make me happy as well as hurt me. That alone made me feel uneasy.

"Shut up and take yo' emotional ass to sleep before I slide up in you and we go for another round," I playfully threatened, grabbing her titties.

She quickly removed my hand. "Oh, hell nawl, I'm good," she protested, moving to her side of the bed. "I don't think my body can handle no more tonight, so you and your penis stay far away from me."

She grabbed the remote to turn off the lights in the room. I got under the sheets and pulled her in the middle of the bed. She tried to fight me away, but I held on to her. "I'm not trying to fuck you, so chill, aight?" Once I said that, her little ass calmed down.

"You better not. I'm not playing with you, Ron," she warned, but it went in one ear and out the other. If I got horny in the middle of the night, I was getting some pussy from her—sleep or not. "What are your feelings on meeting my parents?"

"I don't have any feelings about it. It's just like meeting two regular motherfuckers that just so happen to be your parents."

She let out a breath of frustration. "Can you be normal for once in your life and show other signs of emotions beside anger?"

"I show other signs."

"Like what?"

I humped her butt. "I'm happy when I play in this pussy," I said, laughing.

"I can't with you right now. Goodnight," she said, snuggling against me.

"I knew that would shut your ass up," I replied, kissing her forehead before closing my eyes to catch some Z's.

****

"Come on! Justin and Tori is already at the jet!" I yelled from Sasha's living room. We had planned to leave her house by seven so we could go straight to the airport, but her greedy ass thought it would be a good idea to eat a bunch of tacos last night. Now she was paying for it.

"My stomach is hurting, though," she whined, coming from the back, rubbing her stomach.

I almost felt sorry for her once I saw the pitiful look she had on her face. "Well, the sooner we leave here to make it to the jet, the faster you can lie down in the bed on there," I reasoned.

Since Justin and I were coming along with them, we decided that it would be best if we just took the jet instead of driving like the girls intended. I wasn't fucking with the idea of being in a car for that many damn hours with limited amount of space to move around. That shit was for the birds.

"Can you carry me?"

I looked at her like she had lost her damn mind. "Who the fuck do I look like? I told you not to eat all that shit, but you didn't listen, so now yo' lil' ass gotta suffer the consequences."

She pouted her lips and tried to stomp past me, out the door. I scooped her up as soon as she was close to me. "I thought you said you wasn't going to carry me?" She smiled in victory. I was tempted to drop her ass for grinning so damn hard, but I couldn't do that even if I wanted to. I wasn't about to let her know that, though.

"Shut up before I hold you over the rail and drop yo' ass," I said, walking down the stairs with her in my arms.

She squinted her eyes I me. "You wouldn't."

"Try me," I dared her, looking in her eyes before kissing her lips.

I stopped in my tracks when I saw Amber leaning against my car with a smirk on her face. "Well, ain't this a beautiful sight to see? Girl, I don't know what you did to this nigga to make him act this way over you, but you need to write a book on this shit. I couldn't get this nigga to call me unless he wanted to fuck, but you got him carrying you."

How in the fuck did this bitch know where Sasha lived, and why did she feel comfortable enough to come around me when she knew I wanted her dead? I grew angry just looking at the bitch. She was lucky that my gun was in the car and not on me, or I would've blown her fucking brains out. "Get your stupid ass away from my car before I hurt yo' simple ass," I said, standing Sasha on her feet.

She started laughing uncontrollably like she just heard the funniest shit in the world. "Hurt me?" She stopped laughing. "You already hurt me when you chose that bitch over me." She pointed to Sasha. "What the fuck she have that I don't? I mean, look at me. I am pretty ass fuck, and my body is on point. I have a job, no kids, and I take care of myself. This bitch doesn't hold a fucking candle to me. I look better and dress better than her, and I'm positive that I fuck better than her as well." She looked at Sasha like she wasn't shit before continuing on with her speech. "If you just give me a chance, I can show you that I'm the better option," she begged.

This bitch was certified crazy. I could kick my own ass for fucking with a bitch like her. "This is my last time warning you. Get the fuck from my car before I beat your ass then shoot you afterward," I said, making my way over to choke her ass, but she pulled a gun from behind her back. I froze when I saw that she was pointing the gun in Sasha's direction.

"It's because of this bitch that you don't love me. Everything was going good until she came in the picture, fucking everything up!" she screamed with tears rolling down her face, looking like a deranged person. My heart felt like it was beating out my fucking chest as I looked back and forth between Sasha and Amber. Sasha stood frightened with tears in her eyes. I had to do something to save her. "In order for you to love me, this bitch gotta die."

Without a second thought, I ran to grab the gun from Amber, but it was too late. She had already pulled the trigger.

Pow.

I felt my heart sinking when I turned away and saw Sasha's body fall to the ground.

TO BE CONTINUED...

Looking for a publishing home?

Royalty Publishing House, Where the Royals reside, is accepting submissions for writers in the urban fiction genre. If you're interested, submit the first 3-4 chapters with your synopsis to submissions@royaltypublishinghouse.com.

Check out our website for more information:

www.royaltypublishinghouse.com.

Text ROYALTY to 42828 to join our mailing list!

To submit a manuscript for our review, email us at submissions@royaltypublishinghouse.com

Text RPHCHRISTIAN to 22828 for our CHRISTIAN ROMANCE novels!

Text RPHROMANCE to 22828 for our INTERRACIAL ROMANCE novels!

Get LiT!

Download the LiTeReader app today and enjoy exclusive content, free books, and more

CPSIA information can be obtained
at www.ICGtesting.com
Printed in the USA
LVHW05s0045120418
573117LV00020BC/306/P